"Your brother ruined my sister's life."

Drawing a steadying breath, Sherry said, "Kim shouldn't have done what he did, Scott, but I can't agree that Ellen's marriage won't work out. What would *you* do if you fell in love with someone you considered your social inferior?"

Scott glanced at her mockingly. "I would certainly not deprive myself." His eyes flicked over her, and she flushed as she understood his meaning. "But I certainly wouldn't marry her. As for my sister's marriage, we'll just have to wait and see, won't we?"

"I—I just hope you won't be too hard on her," Sherry murmured.

Scott shrugged, appearing to lose interest in his sister. "I told you, you'd be wiser to worry about yourself."

Remembering Scott's earlier threats, Sherry shivered.

Books by Margaret Pargeter

HARLEQUIN PRESENTS

HARLEQUIN ROMANCE

These books may be available at your local bookseller.

Don't miss any of our special offers. Write to us at the following address for information on our newest releases.

Harlequin Reader Service
P.O. Box 52040, Phoenix, AZ   85072-2040
Canadian address: P.O. Box 2800, Postal Station A,
5170 Yonge St., Willowdale, Ont. M2N 6J3

MARGARET PARGETER

born of the wind

Harlequin Books

TORONTO • NEW YORK • LONDON
AMSTERDAM • PARIS • SYDNEY • HAMBURG
STOCKHOLM • ATHENS • TOKYO • MILAN

Harlequin Presents first edition September 1985
ISBN 0-373-10821-4

Original hardcover edition published in 1984
by Mills & Boon Limited

CHAPTER ONE

SHERRY had been expecting the car, so it was no surprise to hear it coming. The unsurfaced road outside exaggerated the sound of tyres gripping it and through the mesh on the window she could smell the cloud of dust which would travel in the wake of Scott Brady's powerful automobile. It was a wonder he hadn't come in one of his fleet of helicopters! she thought bitterly.

She didn't hear his footsteps approaching. Like a lot of big men he moved quietly, but she would have had to be deaf not to have heard his angry knock on the door. Anger could be conveyed better than most emotions through actions as well as words, and there was no mistaking it in the savage tattoo which invaded the momentary silence. Scott Brady sounded threatening as well as furious.

Though involuntarily Sherry shuddered, her own nervousness somehow helped to stiffen her wavering courage. I'll take no notice until he knocks again, she decided mutinously. Remaining seated at the table, a cup of lukewarm coffee clasped in her shaking hands, she stared at it fixedly, refusing to allow her agitated feet to budge. In another ten seconds—she began counting, I'll go and see what he wants. As if she didn't already know! Ever since Kim had left she had known Scott Brady would turn up. It would be hopeless to pray that he was here for any other reason than that her brother had gone out with his sister.

Sherry didn't have to wait for the second knock. Scott even saved her the bother of answering the door by flinging it open and striding, uninvited into the kitchen!

'Why . . .! How—how dare you?' Sherry stammered,

her long braid of silky dark hair swinging as she jumped
to her feet.

'How dare you sit there ignoring me?' the man
suddenly looming over her countered icily. 'I've a good
mind to put you over my knee and lay into you until
you can't sit down again!'

A strange feeling shot through Sherry as she glared at
him, her sapphire blue eyes shouting defiance in her
small tired face. 'There's no need to be abusive, Mr
Brady! I was on my way,' well, she'd intended to be. 'If
I wasn't fast enough to please you, that's no excuse for
losing your temper.'

'You think not?' he exploded, one hand whipping out
to grasp the two fronts of her shirt, jerking her to
within inches of his furious face. 'Let me tell you, Miss
Grant, I don't appreciate being left to cool my heels on
anyone's doorstep while the lady of the house tries to
decide whether or not she's in!'

Sherry ignored the dangerous quality about Scott
Brady which usually made her think twice before she
spoke. 'I told you!' she hissed, her face scarlet now and
glowing with a temper almost matching his, 'I was on
my way.'

'If that's your normal speed,' he snapped, 'no wonder
this place is going to rack and ruin!'

'That's not true!' she forced herself to deny the
obvious. 'Not that it's any of your business!'

'It shouldn't be,' he agreed cynically.

Feeling irritated beyond endurance, Sherry replied in
much the same tone. 'You don't have to bother
snooping round!'

His thin mouth went tight. 'If it only concerned you
and your brother, I'd have washed my hands of you
long ago. Unfortunately my sister appears to be
involved.'

She swallowed and closed her eyes. So he did know
about Kim and Ellen. Since he had guessed as much, it
was no real surprise, but she hadn't been prepared for

such icy disapproval. With an effort she hung on to her self-control, taking deep, quick breaths in order to prevent herself from losing it completely. A free-for-all with Scott Brady wouldn't help Kim. In the three years since Kim and she had come from England to live with their grandfather on his sheep station in New South Wales, her encounters with Scott Brady, their wealthy neighbour, had been few and far between. It was only since her grandfather had died, six months ago that they had seen more of him. Why, she had no idea. Whenever she mentioned it to Kim, he replied evasively that it might have something to do with Scott wishing to buy the property from him, but Sherry wasn't altogether convinced. If Scott Brady was interested in a property she was sure he would make enquiries through the usual channels, rather than approaching the owner himself.

It was more likely, Sherry suspected, that the frequency of Scott Brady's visits had more to do with an increasing concern for his sister rather than any urgent desire to add Googon to his already outsize empire. That Ellen might be even remotely interested in a man apparently incapable of running even a small station properly must go greatly against the grain. Not that Sherry could altogether blame him, though she would never admit it. Ellen, at twenty-four, was a pleasant and beautiful girl, but she had probably never done a day's work in her life. She just wasn't cut out to be the wife of a struggling sheep farmer who couldn't be classed as even a minor member of the ruling squattocracy!

Scott Brady appeared to have forgotten he still held Sherry by her shirt fronts in the grip of his steely fingers. His cool grey eyes were focused on her face, and feeling scorched by the disparagement of his exploring glance, she suddenly realised how close they were and wrenched away from him. Giving herself a moment to recover from the peculiar sensation contact with his knuckles had aroused on her skin, she pretended to be reflecting on what he had said. Two thoughts were going through her mind and she was confused that she couldn't connect them. It was the first time he had touched her and the first time he had come out in the open regarding his sister.

'I think you're getting things out of proportion, Mr Brady.' She took another deep breath in order to counter the mounting cynicism in his hard, dark face. 'It's not difficult to guess how much you disapprove of me and my brother, but if you're trying to stop Kim and Ellen seeing each other then I'd suggest you're going about it the wrong way.'

His eyes narrowed. Abruptly he asked, 'How old are you?'

She would have staked her last cent he already knew. 'Twenty, almost.'

'Yes,' his nod confirmed her suspicions, 'little more than a child. So you must allow that with my considerable advantage, both in years and experience, my judgment must be vastly superior to yours. Your brother and my sister may believe they're in love, but anything as serious as marriage between them could only end in total disaster. I'd be a fool, we'd both be fools, Miss Grant, if we permitted things to go as far as that. Kim doesn't like work, he doesn't even pretend to, while my sister doesn't know what work is. An alliance between two such people would be frankly impossible.'

Immediately Sherry sprang to her brother's defence. 'Kim does try!' she cried. 'It's not his fault he was brought up in an entirely different environment, but the fact that he doesn't like sheep doesn't prove he'd be a failure as a husband!'

'If he can't make enough to support a wife, he's bound to be a failure as a husband,' Scott retorted dryly.

'Doesn't your own record rather contradict this?' Sherry shot back, too angry to be discreet.

For a moment, as his face froze, she feared he was going to hit her. In the thickness of the sudden silence, she could feel his anger leaping out at her. Scott Brady, according to her grandfather, had been married in his twenties, to the daughter of one of his father's business associates. Their divorce three years later had remained a mystery, the only clear point emerging being the obvious one, that the marriage had failed. Despite the fury in his face, Sherry couldn't help wondering why Scott Brady's marriage hadn't been a success. Still in his middle thirties, he was a handsome, virile man. Surely no woman in love with him would have been willing to let him go?

Just as she expected to feel the weight of his hand across her cheek, his anger seemed to fade and he merely shrugged indifferently. 'My marriage needn't concern you. Let's concentrate on your brother.'

Sherry bit her lip sharply. He wasn't prepared to discuss his marriage, to make comparisons, and she must accept it. But she wouldn't, she vowed, do anything to help him demolish the growing friendship between Kim and Ellen.

'Your affairs don't interest me as much as your theories,' she replied coolly. 'I was only trying to point out that you can't generalise about everything, and that money doesn't necessarily guarantee happiness. I suggest, if you want Kim and Ellen to forget each other, you should try leaving them alone. It's quite probably your antagonism that's driving them on.'

He laughed sarcastically. 'So far as theories go, that must be more old hat than any of mine. You can't really be suggesting that I should encourage them to imagine I approve of what's going on?'

'Would it be such a bad thing?' she asked, suddenly weary.

'A bad thing?' His tone implied she was witless. 'It would be a tragedy, pommie girl.'

'So that's it!' As anger dispersed the tiredness she felt,

her blue eyes sparked rage at him. 'Since Kim and I came to live with Grandfather, you've never accepted us, have you? After he died you stopped even pretending to! We're still pommies because we haven't been notably successful. If ever we are, you might just accept us as Australians, but until that day arrives we remain foreigners!'

Scott Brady regarded her impassively throughout the whole of her impassioned speech, obviously unmoved by it. 'It happens all over the world.'

Bitterly she retorted, 'So you admit it?'

He said abruptly, his eyes glinting, 'I don't consider you and your brother no good, but if Kim had the guts to try harder it might make a hell of a difference. Respect has to be earned, and I reckon this applies to the whole universe, not just this particular corner of it.'

'You have to give him time!' she protested fiercely. 'He's learning fast.'

'To let his sister do all the work,' he tacked on bitingly.

The derision in his voice made Sherry shiver. 'I don't . . .'

'You do!'

'You can't know that!' she gasped.

Meeting her widening glance contemptuously, he snapped, 'I know all right.'

He probably did. Men like him frequently saw too much! Staring at him resentfully, Sherry collapsed in her chair again, her legs feeling suddenly weak. 'I like being outside,' she muttered. 'I enjoy riding. Grandfather was never keen to let me . . .'

'He kept you hard at it in here, didn't he?' Scott interrupted. 'He made a slave of you to keep you out of mischief. He would have done better to have paid more attention to your brother.'

Sherry frowned. 'He didn't want me running off as my mother did. I can understand that, but he also taught Kim a lot.'

'Tried to!' Scott muttered tauntingly.

'Mr Brady!' Sherry was swiftly on her feet again, her face flushing wildly. 'I see no point in continuing this conversation. You haven't convinced me, nor are you likely to, that I have any right to interfere in my brother's life—at least, not concerning the girls he takes out. And if he chooses to be friendly with your sister, who are you to judge if he's good enough for her or not?'

Scott Brady's eyes glittered so coldly, Sherry found herself on the verge of retracting what she had said. It took a lot of courage to continue defying him, but she hoped he was aware of how little real influence she had over Kim. Kim was six years older and their parents had always spoiled him. He had been their golden boy, she only the dark, rather secretive young daughter who didn't count.

'You little fool,' she was jerked rudely back to reality as Scott ground out, 'why do you still refuse to face facts?'

Sherry flinched as he attacked her while the colour deepened in her cheeks. 'Mr Brady!' she spluttered indignantly, 'if I were to agree to do as you ask, how would you expect me to go about splitting Kim and Ellen up? I'm no magician. I wouldn't even know where to start!'

'Whoever reared you,' he snapped—she thought unreasonably, 'failed to knock any sense into your head. If we stuck together—I believe the word is collaborate—we might achieve a lot.'

'No!' She felt immediate apprehension, as every instinct warned her, for her own sake as well as Kim's, against any closer contact with this man. 'I——' she stammered, 'I still think you have no right to interfere in something that's none of your business!'

'Sherry,' he retorted grimly, 'I'm getting tired of standing here, hearing you repeatedly telling me that. My sister is surely my business. I have to take care of her, and if you refuse to take my word for it, I'll have to find another way of proving just how unsuitable a match between your brother and her would be.'

'Another way?' Sherry voiced in nervous confusion.

'Yes,' in a flash he was by her side, his hand on her arm this time, 'you're coming with me.'

'With you?'

They were halfway over the kitchen before she belatedly realised what was happening and dug her heels in. To her incredulous surprise, as he felt her resistance, Scott turned, swinging her up in his arms, his powerful frame accepting her slight weight easily. Before she could pull herself together sufficiently to fight him, they were outside and he was lowering her into the front seat of the car, then driving off with her.

Automatically Sherry's hand flew to the door.

'It's locked,' Scott said coolly.

Sherry heard her breath draw in like a sob. 'Just what do you think you're doing?' she gasped.

'Taking you to Coomarlee,' he replied mockingly. 'You haven't been.'

Blindly, she tried to steady her whirling senses and uneven pulse. She had been held close in Scott Brady's arms, but surely not close enough to feel so entirely disorientated? As shock waves trembled through her bones, she thought she might faint. Confusion reigned in what little coherent thought remained. It must be fear, a dread of the unknown, that was making her react so peculiarly.

'No,' she agreed breathlessly, when she was at last able to speak, 'I haven't been to Coomarlee, and I have no desire to go. I'm ordering you to turn round and take me straight home again, Mr Brady.'

He laughed dismissively, without taking his eyes off the dusty track. 'If you'd agreed to do as I asked, in the first place, none of this might have been necessary.'

Bewildered, Sherry stared at him, deriving little comfort from the chiselled hardness of his profile.

'How is taking me to Coomarlee going to alter the situation?'

'It might not,' he rejoined curtly, 'but at least it will give you some idea of Ellen's life style. You'll see how she's used to living and be able to compare it with what your brother has to offer. I realise,' he went on smoothly, 'how it might be impossible for someone from an ordinary background to imagine the difference.'

Sherry thought she must have gasped more in the past half hour than she had done in weeks! 'I always believed there were no snobs in Australia!' she exclaimed sarcastically.

'In this instance I'd rather call it common sense,' he countered coolly.

Appearing quite satisfied, when she made no reply, that he had had the last word, Scott fell silent. Sherry was silent because she didn't know what to say, then decided it might be better not to say anything.

Dazed, she gazed through the car window at the golden plains over which they were travelling. They lived not far from Bourke, a town almost eight hundred miles north-west of Sydney, which was a service centre for a vast area of outback sheep country. She liked Australia, she supposed her roots were here as her grandparents had been born here, but this evening her eyes were somehow blind to the land she had grown to love.

Scott Brady must have no idea her father had been a wealthy financier. Sherry knew that her grandfather had quarrelled with her parents after they had married and her English father had refused to come and live on the station. Her mother had once told her that despite many attempts on her part, the quarrel had never been patched up, and the last time she had seen him he had sworn never to allow her name to pass his lips again. Sherry realised he couldn't have done, for when she and her brother had arrived at Googon no one seemed to have been aware of their existence. It was immediately assumed they were a pair of poor orphans. They had been, of course, after their parents had gone down with their yacht in the Aegean, just before the crash.

How John Carey had learned about it, he would never say, but within weeks of it happening, when he might have almost uncannily guessed how desperate Kim was to escape the repercussions of financial ruin and the ridicule of his so-called friends, he had sent for them. His treatment of them had been fair, but so harsh that Sherry suspected that any softer emotions no longer had a place in his life. Often she felt he was taking revenge for their mother's defection, but she had never minded as much as Kim. What she had minded was her grandfather's and Kim's determination never to speak of her parents. Both the two men had given the impression that they only wished to forget, an attitude which, though in some ways sensible, hurt Sherry a lot. She could understand them being bitter, but she had hoped that Kim would eventually forgive his parents, especially his mother.

John Carey, she thought, had taken more to Kim than herself. Once, after putting up with his constant grousing for days, she had asked him why she was unable to please him. He had answered that she looked too much like his daughter, who had abused the freedom he had given her by marrying a man who had refused to live here and help him.

It had been useless trying to argue that her father hadn't been cut out to be a grazier. She was sure Richard Grant would never have settled happily away from his beloved London and had more sense than to comment on his financial success, much in evidence before everything had gone wrong. She remembered their beautiful homes, both in London and the country, but she knew if she mentioned them her grandfather would believe she was still yearning for them.

At barely seventeen she had been young to look back

over much, but she hadn't found the transition from her former life to this one easy. Yet after a painful period of settling in she began loving this part of Australia quite fiercely. She would have settled quite happily on Googon if her grandfather had given her the least encouragement. Even without this, she never had any thought of running away. Kim had proved the restless one and it had become a habit to think he only needed time.

John Carey's station, which he had left entirely to Kim, was small compared to that of Scott Brady's. His was huge, covering over forty thousand hectares, and, according to John Carey, there wasn't a better run place! Scott's father had apparently neglected it, but after Scott had inherited he had made a lot of changes. Sherry had heard that the complex around the house was like a small village, while the house itself was well able to take one's breath away. All this Sherry had yet to see, for Scott Brady seemingly didn't issue invitations to his poorer neighbours, especially anti-social ones like her grandfather. She had only met Ellen Brady through Kim, and then it had been on Googon, not Coomarlee.

Neither Scott or Sherry spoke until they reached Coomarlee. This part of New South Wales, through which ran the meandering Darling River, was hot and barren for most of the year. The winter climate, from the end of March to November, was bracing and pleasant, but otherwise the heat and dust could be trying. For some the monotony of seemingly endless plains and low, rocky ranges interspersed by slow-flowing rivers had no attraction, but for Sherry, each day brought an increasing fascination. If she had been apprehensive over leaving London, now she had an even greater fear of having to leave Googon and perhaps never seeing it again.

Most of the roads being rough and unsealed, Sherry was used to bumping over them. She was relieved to see the buildings of Scott's property loom in view, chiefly because she had a great desire to get what she guessed might be an ordeal over and done with. Nevertheless, her first glimpse of his home impressed her.

At Googon and other similar places, the homestead was built on the track with nothing but a width of dusty ground between it and the veranda. Here it was different. The Brady homestead was surrounded by irrigated paddocks which considerably softened the landscape between the house and the red plains beyond it. The house itself was a superb affair, two-storied and gracious, shaded by trees and well laid out gardens which Sherry knew contained a magnificent pool. Ellen had once said they used it a lot to entertain visitors. There would be no hasty dipping in boreholes here as they did at Googon!

As the last mile or two of track was hard, Sherry scarcely realised when Scott drew up in front of the house. Dazedly she blinked as he quickly dragged her from the car and swept her inside.

'A conducted tour, I think,' he said curtly, continuing to drag her around.

Aware that the point of the exercise was to make her conscious of the difference between Coomarlee and Googon, Sherry made no attempt to escape the hand clamped on her arm like a steel trap. He was determined that his total disapproval of any possible alliance between Kim and his sister should be backed by all the evidence he could produce that Ellen would never survive in a less than luxurious environment.

What he didn't know was that Sherry had once lived in comparable luxury herself. Any one of her father's houses might have easily matched the expensive interior of this. If she ever told him it would only be as a last resort, to convince him it was possible to survive a change from luxury to more basic conditions. If she could do it surely Ellen could, especially with the help she could expect from Kim, as her husband.

They appeared to have the house to themselves, even

the kitchen was empty. Sherry sensed that even after the sheer size and opulence of the other rooms, Scott considered this one of his trump cards.

'We have a housekeeper,' he said briefly, 'but if we hadn't this is the kind of equipment Ellen would have at her disposal.'

Sherry glanced at the huge expanse of gleaming tiles and stainless steel, which must be every housewife's dream, containing every piece of modern equipment imaginable. Her eyes suddenly shimmered as she saw her mother discussing with the cook the menu for an important dinner party.

In the grip of an unexpected wave of nostalgia, she surrendered, whispering unevenly, 'I see what you mean. The kitchen at Googon is nothing like this.'

'Exactly!'

Although she flushed with humiliation at Scott's dry disparagement, she refused to drop her head. The kitchen at Googon, in which she had struggled daily for the past three years to feed innumerable men, was a far cry from the one she was standing in now. To begin with, the huge, wood-burning stove had nearly broken her back as well as her heart. Many tears she had wept over it. Still, it did cook wonderfully when it was in the right mood and somehow gave more satisfaction than a modern cooker which worked at the mere flick of a switch!

The tour ended in the grounds, which proved every bit as impressive as the house. When it was concluded, Scott brought her back to the kitchens again, where for the first time he let go of her to make coffee.

'I would offer you a drink,' he said, 'but you look as if you have got an empty stomach.'

Sherry was surprised that he noticed such things of those he considered inferior! Moodily, she rubbed the arm which bore the imprint of his fingers, wondering if she would ever get rid of the burning feeling. It seemed hours since she had served the men their dinner and

somehow forgotten to eat herself. There weren't many
men left, just old Sam and his son, since Kim had
discovered Googon was heavily mortgaged and they
had practically no money.

She didn't realise she was hungry until she began
eating the thick ham sandwiches Scott cut, but as she
nibbled, she still pondered on why a man like the
master of Coomarlee should need the help of a girl like
herself over anything. He was obviously a man used to
ruling alone and being more than capable of doing so!

She was driven to comment. 'I can't understand why
you should need my assistance. Isn't your so-called
problem with Ellen something you could settle
yourself?'

His steely eyes bored into her. 'Believe me, Miss
Grant, there isn't much I'm not capable of dealing with
myself. I'm not in the habit of running to strangers each
time I have a family problem.'

She made another attempt. 'Have you tried talking to
Ellen?'

His brows lifted tersely. 'Since I discovered she's
thinking of marrying your brother, yes.'

'M-marrying . . .?'

As Sherry's voice stammered and faded in sheer
astonishment, Scott's deepened in irony. 'Don't tell me
you had no idea!'

Sherry gulped for air. Before Scott's arrival that
evening, it had never occurred to her that Kim could be
thinking seriously of marriage. She still felt slightly
incredulous. 'I hadn't,' she gasped. 'Neither of them
said anything to me.'

Scott's voice hardened perceptibly. 'So you're
sticking to the theory that you hadn't a clue?'

His unfairness had a bracing effect. 'I'm not good at
guessing games, Mr Brady. Just because a couple go out
together a few times it doesn't necessarily mean they're
in love with each other.'

He ignored this. 'Maybe you were too busy hoping

something would come of it to question the wisdom of it? Kim married to my sister and living at Coomarlee might bring comparable benefits to yourself. You might expect to share everything he hopes will come his way if he marries into a wealthy family.'

'You're ridiculous!' she cried, her face hot with indignation. 'And insulting!'

'I'm merely speaking plainly, Miss Grant.'

They stared at each other like enemies, the tall, powerful man, the trembling girl. 'If you've only just noticed Ellen's involvement with my brother,' Sherry choked, 'is it fair to insist that I should have been more observant?'

Curtly he bit out, 'I've been away a lot lately, Miss Grant, and, contrary to what you might think, when I am here I rarely play the heavy parent. Ellen is my sister, and though I was left in charge of her, we lead separate lives. With certain stipulations, I allow her to choose her own friends, and I haven't time to vet them all. Her marriage, however, is another thing. When it comes to choosing a husband, a girl needs a guiding hand.'

Sherry spluttered at such arrogance. 'Don't you believe in love?'

'It soon fades—if such a thing exists beyond mere physical attraction.'

'Kim isn't that handsome.'

'He has enough,' the relentless voice went on, 'to blind a girl's eyes to the weakness underneath.'

'How dare you!' Sherry's eyes blazed. She wished she was a man so she could knock the expression of taunting derision off Scott Brady's face. 'You believe Kim and I are out for all we can get and are no good!'

'You took advantage of your grandfather's generosity.'

'You call it—that?'

'What else?'

His eyes narrowed again on her face, as if something

about it held his attention despite himself. Sherry wasn't a big girl, she could be more accurately described as petite. When she first came to Googon, her cheeks had still had a babyish roundness, but since then her face had thinned, revealing exotic bone structure. Now the delicate lines of her face made her brilliant blue eyes seem huge and, combined with her high cheekbones, gave her an almost Eastern quality. She had become—and it would have been more obvious, had she been suitably dressed—a young woman both striking and unusual. Properly dressed and groomed she would stand out in a crowd, something which suddenly seemed to occur to the man watching her. Her fragile neck supported a proud little head and her slender figure might be nothing less than seductive. She was dark, whereas Kim was fair, but as though something about her reminded Scott Brady of her brother, his hard lips thinned decisively.

Unaware of his appraisal, Sherry muttered bleakly, 'If Grandfather was over-benevolent we never noticed.'

'Gratitude didn't blind you,' he retorted sarcastically.

Sherry shrugged, making no further attempt to defend herself. It was his attitude towards Kim which was causing her anxiety. For all their parents had spoiled him, she was convinced life had given him a raw deal, she didn't know what he would do if things got worse. Scott Brady couldn't know what it was like to have everything you'd grown up to believe in and depend on swept away from you, but she refused to believe that Kim was looking for someone to supply what he had lost.

As she gazed stubbornly at Scott Brady, a part of her mind became engrossed at the way their eyes sparked together. Only during the last few minutes had she noticed how increasingly difficult it was becoming, when he looked at her, to tear her eyes away from his silvery grey ones. His glance was magnetic, holding hers captive, the results far from comfortable. He seemed to be drawing her towards him, depriving her of a will of her own.

Incredulous that her feet were actually edging forward, Sherry stumbled as she jerked back. Righting herself, she regained her composure but now levelled her gaze no higher than his shirt buttons.

With an effort, she concentrated on his oblique accusations. 'We aren't all mercenary, Mr Brady, but I don't intend offering proof. I will say one thing, I would hate Kim to be any part of such a cynical family. Ellen is nice, but if she allows herself to be overruled by you, Kim would be better off without her.'

'I'm sure he would be,' very smoothly. 'I'm glad you're beginning to show sense.'

Amazed how he had picked from her heated tirade only what suited him, Sherry dared not raise her eyes from the breadth of his chest to scornfully challenge him. In fact her capacity to thwart him at all appeared to be leaving her. Had he usually this effect on people? she wondered dazedly. 'What must I do?' she whispered agitatedly, soft colour flowing under her skin. 'I haven't a clue—you must forgive me. Interfering in the affairs of others isn't a habit of mine.'

He ignored her obvious sarcasm. 'I want you to ring me every time Ellen appears on your doorstep.'

'Just that?'

'For the time being. You might point out, whenever you get the chance, to both Ellen and your brother, that she is used to better things than he can supply.'

Scott's eyes penetrated the top of her head and something about his chest was affecting her adversely. Or was it his words that were causing the turmoil? Subduing a returning desire to defy him, she restrained herself to suggesting dryly, 'Why don't you invite Kim here, Mr Brady, and give him the same treatment as you're giving me? Invite a bunch of your friends, too, and let Ellen make comparisons. A few beautiful girls,' she added recklessly, 'might even succeed in diverting Kim's attention from Ellen permanently.'

She was startled, perhaps because of his air of uncompromising male authority, that he appeared to be listening to what she said. 'Would you come too?' he asked.

'I'd rather not,' she declined politely.

He shrugged, as if it was of no importance. 'It's an idea, as long as we can keep a sense of proportion. I have no intention of allowing this whole thing to be reduced to the level of comic opera. Nor have I the inclination to spend more time than necessary on this unfortunate affair. If your brother doesn't stop pursuing Ellen very quickly, I shall remove her from his immediate vicinity.'

Such ruthlessness could only be infuriating. Up came Sherry's head. 'Why don't you do that now, Mr Brady?' she asked sharply.

He met the blaze of her blue eyes without giving an inch. 'Because I would rather she was cured of her infatuation beforehand. Otherwise such an exercise might easily defeat its own purpose.'

Such logic was again infuriating, but Sherry could see he was a master at pleading his own case. Ramming it down her throat, more likely, if she didn't at least appear to accept what he was talking about! Stiffly she agreed, 'I'll do what I can. Now would you take me home, please?'

CHAPTER TWO

THE return journey to Googon was conducted as silently as that of the one an hour previously. Scott, his mission accomplished, wasn't bothering with polite conversation. Sherry supposed he imagined the battle over his sister as good as won and was settling contentedly to his own business again.

Casting a hostile glance at his strong profile, she allowed that he was a fabulous-looking man. There was a strength about him which must be comforting for those who basked under his protection, but a little too much strength for the unfortunates who choose to make an enemy of him. At thirty-six, Scott Brady was as hard and unyielding as the area he lived in, the charm and great intelligence merely a façade to hide an arrogantly dictatorial personality. Women, it was rumoured, were fascinated by him, and while Sherry was receiving vague telepathic notions as to why this should be, she refused to believe she was anything other than repulsed by him. Her one aim in life, from now on, might easily be to take him down a peg or two. Although she doubted this would be at all possible, even to think of it made her feel better.

Such flights of fancy had to be curtailed, of course. It was like a beggarmaid threatening a king! Thinking of Scott Brady in such terms might not be sensible, but Sherry's memories of England were still quite vivid and she could never recall seeing anyone to match him. Nor here, for that matter; though imprisoned on her grandfather's station, she hadn't met many men.

When Scott dropped her off, he said briefly, 'I'll be in touch.'

She wasn't conscious of being enveloped in dust as he

23

whipped round and drove off. Not until a piece of grit hit her eye, did she realise she was standing motionless, gazing after him.

After stumbling to the kitchen and extracting the piece of grit, she got on with the washing up that Scott had interrupted. She couldn't help wondering why she hadn't been anywhere as near conscious of him before. True, they had never mixed socially, but his presence on Googon wasn't unknown. Perhaps it was because she was usually in the kitchen that they had so seldom actually met.

No matter how hard she polished glasses, her thoughts refused to leave him, the reason for his visit, this evening, bringing a frown. She couldn't remember when Kim had begun taking Ellen out. They might have been going out together for a while before she noticed, for Kim often disappeared of an evening without saying where he was going or who with. Not even when Ellen had taken to calling occasionally had she suspected there was anything serious going on. She had believed Ellen was merely passing an idle hour; certainly it had never occurred to her that the other girl could be falling in love with Kim.

Was she? Sherry wondered. Mightn't she have said she wanted to marry Kim in order to provoke her brother? Scott probably ordered her round as arrogantly as he did everyone else, and Ellen might have retaliated in a way she knew would annoy him most. Sherry hung up her tea-towel and decided not to worry too much until she'd had a word with Kim in the morning.

At ten the next morning, while she was still trying to find a tactful way of broaching the subject, Ellen rang with an invitation.

Kim answered the phone. He was late coming down for breakfast. The men had already left for far pastures after eating the succulent lamb chops Sherry had cooked them at five o'clock. He returned from the phone looking dazed. Immediately Sherry thought of Coomarlee and went tense.

'That takes some beating!' he muttered, ignoring his half eaten breakfast but picking up his coffee cup, his jerky movements betraying his total surprise.

'What does?'

Sherry's voice turned his head in her direction. It was then she saw he had gone pale. 'An invitation to Coomarlee, after all this time.'

'An—invitation?' She had to pretend she had no idea what he was talking about, to be as astonished as he was. 'What kind of invitation?'

Kim frowned broodingly, as if he couldn't decide himself. 'They're giving a dinner party.'

'So?' Sherry had to be flippant to hide her true reaction. She had never expected Scott to act on her suggestion. 'That's no big deal, is it? You've been to plenty.'

'Before we came here.'

Noticing his tenseness, she was at a loss as to how to cope with it. Forcing another smile, she said lightly, 'At least you know better than to eat your peas with a knife.'

'Sherry, for God's sake!' he snapped, his face darkening morosely. 'Can't you see? Scott Brady's an autocrat who thinks I'm a tramp. Isn't it enough to make a saint suspicious that he should suddenly ask me to his home?'

Sherry seized the opportunity, feeling like a traitor to her own brother. 'Can you think of any particular reason why he should issue such an invitation?'

'I might if I tried,' Kim replied enigmatically, 'but I have no wish to.'

She persevered, 'You've been taking Ellen out. Perhaps he likes being sociable to her friends?'

'That would be the day!' Kim exclaimed sarcastically. 'Discrimination's Mr Brady's middle name! If our papa hadn't gone broke he might have treated me differently, but he doesn't ordinarily let blokes like me over his doorstep.'

Her own sentiments exactly!—and how true. 'I realise no one knows anything about us,' she began awkwardly, 'but have you never thought of telling Ellen?'

'No!' he broke in tersely. 'What would be the use?'

The bitterness in his face woke her sympathy. 'Ellen once said she guessed from the way we talked that we had come from a nice family. It was when Grandfather was alive and I daren't say anything . . .'

'She told me the same thing,' his mouth creased with cynical amusement, 'I said Papa had been butler to a duke.'

'You—didn't!'

Sherry's horrified astonishment was tinged with hysterical amusement when he nodded carelessly. 'I've always had a hankering to be loved for myself alone.'

Curiously, Sherry studied him. Somehow she hadn't noticed before he was extremely attractive. He might not quite have Scott Brady's brand of looks, but he was tall and fairly well made. There was an appealing air of boyishness about him which a lot of girls might fall for. Usually, she had to admit, her brother was easy to get on with, but there was something about him which occasionally disturbed her, a streak of recklessness, a determination to gratify his own needs at the expense of others that she couldn't approve. It often showed, she realised, in the way he frequently left the men to do the work while he sneaked off and enjoyed himself.

As always, she assured herself he just needed time, though for once she didn't indulge him completely. 'Ellen, any girl,' she said with gentle irony, 'would have to love you to settle for this. You have to be fair.'

Kim flushed. 'I'm not thinking of bringing anyone here. Ellen's all right, but I wish her brother didn't interfere.'

'He might stop, if you accept his invitation and make a good impression? Who did you speak to on the phone, by the way?'

'Ellen.'

'I see.' For a moment Sherry had thought it might have been Scott himself. 'You'll be going?'

'Naturally,' he grinned mirthlessly. 'I may not get another chance.'

'When is it?' asked Sherry.

'Tomorrow.'

'Tomorrow?' Sherry frowned. Scott wasn't wasting any time!

'You're invited too.'

'Oh, no!' she almost jumped as Kim spoke. She couldn't! She had asked to be excluded and Scott had agreed. What mischief was he up to now? 'I hope you told Ellen I had other things to do?'

'I tried to—I mean,' Kim muttered somewhat uncomfortably, 'I knew you wouldn't be keen, but she insisted that her brother said both of us. You'd better come, for my sake.'

'I'll press your suit,' she said tonelessly, suffering slightly from shock. 'They'll probably expect us to turn up in jeans.'

'Ellen didn't say.'

'She'll take it for granted.' Sherry still felt betrayed. 'You have to realise she's used to that kind of thing. It would never occur to her that we all don't have a rig-out for every occasion.'

'You're really rubbing it in, aren't you?' His brows dropped suspiciously. 'I wonder why?'

Sherry couldn't tell him. It was strange how she was following Scott's dictation to the letter! He might have cast a spell on her from all those miles away. Things were certainly impinging on her mind from somewhere. Evasively she replied, 'If you're getting serious about Ellen, Mr Brady might not be pleased?'

Kim grimaced. 'Am I in the position to be serious over any girl? Maybe I just like giving Mr Brady something to think about? Ellen and I bumped into him one day in Bourke and he'd never been so mad that he could remember! Of course he hid it.'

'What—what did he do?'

Kim grinned with bitter satisfaction. 'He couldn't actually do very much. He was with a blonde and I had Ellen. A brawl in the street wouldn't be his style, anyway, though I've heard he wasn't above it when he was younger. But that's why I can't understand him issuing invitations. Is he thirsting for a chance to put me in my place, or is he offering an olive branch?'

Sherry wasn't listening. 'Who was the blonde?'

'Kingston Easten's daughter'—he named a leading politician. 'Some dame!'

Kim frequently used Americanisms, when he felt alienated from the U.K. and Australia. Sherry prayed he wasn't having one of his antagonistic spells now. 'Don't do anything stupid tomorrow evening,' she begged.

'You'd better come and see I don't,' he advised sarcastically.

Sherry realised he meant it. Under the bravado, something was troubling him, making him nervous. Concern for him being always uppermost, she nodded reluctantly. 'All right, I'll come. I don't know what I'll wear though. I might need a new dress.'

This was no exaggeration, but she wasn't surprised when Kim instantly looked dismayed. 'Surely you brought plenty from England?'

'We could only bring so much,' she reminded him. 'And you grabbed most of the space.'

'Did I?' He sounded vaguely apologetic. 'You had a dress for the old man's funeral.'

Sherry sighed at his careless reference to their grandfather, who had left him all he had. 'The best of what I have.'

'It will do. I really can't afford you another,' Kim said sulkily. 'We lost a lot of stock in those bush fires and the mortgage has to be paid. We'll be lucky if there's enough to pay for the absolute necessities and the mens wages.'

She might have mentioned that letting their insurances lapse hadn't paid off in the long run, but she knew better. 'Mr Brady might not approve if I turn up minus a sweeping evening gown.'

'He will have to accept it.'

Would he? On their way to Coomarlee, the following evening, Sherry asked herself the same question again. She had tried to get hold of Scott Brady. Twice she had secretly rung his house without success, and, yesterday, she had ridden out to the far paddocks, braving the heat of the midday sun in an attempt to find him. She knew he spent a lot of time actually working with his staff, but there had been no sign of him in the places where she had occasionally caught glimpses of him before. She had returned to the homestead with a heavy heart and aching head.

Sherry bit her lip as she glanced at her brother driving the old truck which served as a car and many other things. Kim was more than passable, his white shirt and tie immaculate, his suit tailored by the best London could offer, paid for by their parents while they had been alive. Sherry had got it out of mothballs, but it would have kept its shape even if the cloth had been in holes. What would Scott make of it? He couldn't accuse her of misleading him, not on the evidence of one suit. If he did, she could always tell him Kim had picked it up second-hand, but knowing she had deliberately set out to trick him didn't make her feel any better. She felt she had gained an invitation to Coomarlee under false pretences, and, knowing Scott Brady, she was apprehensive as to what his reactions might be.

Perhaps her own appearance would convince him that Kim's seeming affluence wasn't what it appeared to be. Wryly her glance fell to the short dress she was wearing. The few long ones she had owned, she had left in London. Her mother had promised her a complete new wardrobe for her seventeenth birthday, but when

the day had arrived she had been here. Most of her
clothes had been sold, along with their homes, to satisfy
greedy creditors, this according to Kim. Why creditors
should so often be referred to as greedy when they were
perfectly within their rights to expect to be repaid what
was owing them, Sherry had never been able to
understand.

The blue dress was neat—it was the best that could
be said of it. Her high-heeled sandals, the only
expensive item she had allowed herself to hang on to,
didn't quite match, but she hadn't been able to resist
the opportunity to wear them. Besides—anxiously she
lifted a small, arched foot—what else could she have
worn? She had done her best, washing her thick, dark
hair and brushing it dry until it resembled a shimmering
cloud when she moved, waving long and gleaming over
her shoulders. The small amount of make-up she had
used added a muted glow to her already lovely skin
while accentuating its pink and white tones. She never
tanned, although she did nothing to prevent it, and
tonight she felt oddly grateful. Her nose was slightly
tilted, her mouth perhaps a little too wide. Her vivid
blue eyes with their dark lashes and feathery brows
were possibly her best feature. They were set like jewels
in a face already enhanced by wonderful bone structure.

'You're a pretty girl. I hadn't realised,' Kim had
joked clumsily when she was ready. 'No one might
notice that dress isn't a new model.'

His attempted humour had lightened the atmosphere,
though he didn't say much more during the miles to
Coomarlee. The plains about them stretched red in the
setting sun, full of the wild, lonely horizons which had
first stolen Sherry's heart. It bred tough men, or
perhaps only the tough survived. She looked at Kim,
thought of Scott Brady and shivered.

Coomarlee shone with lights, streaming out from
every window. Again Sherry was struck by the grandeur
of the place. Scott had shown her over the house, but

grouped behind it were all the other buildings which could turn an outback station into a small village.

Inside the house, this evening, there appeared to be crowds of people. Having led a very secluded life for so long, Sherry naturally felt somewhat out of her depth to start with. She didn't notice individuals among the sea of faces, but she did get a general impression of women in long dresses and magnificently turned out men. Obviously Scott Brady wasn't a man who believed in half-measures. He intended showing the Grants up and was going to do it in style! Her former remorse at deceiving him gone, Sherry lifted her head proudly and walked forward. Kim was all right, she was the one who would stand out. Mr Brady was entitled to be annoyed if his plan misfired, but she tried not to let this disturb her!

Ellen rushed to meet them, her brother, animating more lean elegance than a panther, followed more slowly. Sherry glanced at him quickly, then looked away again.

'Kim!' There could be no mistaking Ellen's welcome. She was wearing green, which complemented red hair, skilfully tinted. Sherry wondered how much it had cost and despised herself for getting into the habit of putting a price on everything.

Scott Brady was an imposing sight, his tailor every bit as good as Kim's, but he was clearly wary. Some comment on Sherry's beauty reached his ears and his tightened mouth indicated anger rather than approval.

She could read his thoughts, or imagined she could. Kim, handsome and very properly attired, was doing nothing to discourage Ellen. He was marking down Sherry's intelligence, writing off entertaining on such a lavish scale as a sheer waste of time and money!

Adroitly but ruthlessly he manoeuvred Sherry aside, noting, how, despite being so shabbily dressed, her slender figure, moving with incredible grace drew all eyes. So different was she, this evening, from the girl he was used to that his forceful jaw set in an unyielding chin, hardened threateningly.

Thrusting a glass of champagne in her hands, he ignored the curious glances. 'I don't usually miss much,' he grated, for her ears alone, 'but I didn't think it was part of the plan to dress your brother up like a Christmas tree. Ellen's besotted enough as it is.'

'His idea, not mine,' Sherry retorted defensively, touching her fastidious little nose to the bubbles in the champagne.

As she lifted her chin defiantly, he suddenly stared at her. She had the soul-shaking feeling that his eyes were trapped by her face. A muscle moved in his cheek and she saw his nostrils flare on a sharp breath.

'Scott, darling!'

Almost gratefully, Sherry thought in surprise, for he was a man who wouldn't appreciate unexpected interruptions, he turned to the blonde vision approaching. Swiftly he introduced her as Miss Easten, then left them together to greet some late arrivals.

Sherry, having guessed from Kim's description of her who Miss Easten was, wasn't pleased to be left in her clutches. Dulcie Easten had quite a vindictive air about her and Sherry was coming in for her fair share of it. She didn't like competition one bit, not even the slightest suspicion of it. It was clear to Sherry that Miss Easten intended changing her name to Brady as soon as she was able and was making sure everyone knew it!

As Scott excused himself, she purred softly, 'Did you think we were holding a fancy-dress party, Miss Grant?'

Sherry, off guard, flushed but made no attempt to prevaricate. 'No, Miss Easten, I didn't.'

'Quite fascinating!' Dulcie went on studying Sherry as though she had stepped out of a museum. 'Do you know Scott well?'

'We're neighbours, actually,' Sherry drawled, thinking there was no reason why Miss Easten shouldn't be got at a little too. She couldn't think of anything more unlikely than Scott looking her way, but Miss Easten was clearly suspicious of any other female within miles of him.

'Neighbours!' as Dulcie's voice rose shrilly, Sherry was relieved when Ellen rescued her. When it came to serious combat, she admitted to being no match for the likes of Dulcie Easten. A little sparring, perhaps, but nothing more serious.

Like her brother, Ellen drew her aside. 'I love your dress.'

Dear me! It was at least getting a lot of attention! 'Are you trying to please me or Kim?' Sherry teased.

'Well, both,' confessed Ellen, flushing guiltily, and in a way which made Sherry glance at her uneasily. Could Scott Brady be right in thinking his sister's feelings were becoming seriously involved? Sherry hadn't thought it possible, now she wasn't so sure.

Ellen put her arm through hers when dinner was announced almost immediately. After finding Kim they trooped into the dining-room together. Sherry said nothing about being here previously, although she could tell Ellen wondered why she wasn't more impressed.

Scott sat at the head of the long, gleaming table, flanked by Miss Easten and another beautiful woman. She was aware that he had chosen his guests carefully, from people who considered themselves the élite! She didn't have to be brilliant to guess his intention had been to subject Kim and herself to the harder edge of society and could scarcely hide her satisfaction to observe how his well laid schemes were going awry. Kim was more than holding his own, and she wasn't the only one to feel proud of him, Ellen was radiant!

At the same time, Sherry was conscious of some qualms going through her. It was one thing to feel triumphant over small victories like this, but quite another to pretend all Scott's doubts about Ellen and her brother were nonsense. No matter how she tried she couldn't see Kim being able to support a wife for years yet. It could mean misery for the three of them if he was to marry Ellen and bring her to Googon.

Catching Scott's glance, she gained no comfort from its calculating blankness. Sitting between two elderly men inclined to be fatherly, she wondered if he had placed her so deliberately. For her sins had he decided she wasn't going to enjoy herself if he could help it. Glances from younger men might be hitting her in waves, but he had nicely isolated her from any closer contact with them.

After dinner and the inevitable coffee, the younger members of the party converged on the pool. 'It's too hot for dancing,' laughed Ellen. 'Let's swim?'

The pool, almost Olympic-size, looked inviting. It had been a hot day and the temperatures hadn't noticeably fallen. Sherry eyed the pool wistfully. Her flesh, overheated by Scott's frequent, enigmatical glances longed for its coolness.

'I haven't a costume,' she explained, when Ellen asked if she wasn't coming to change.

'No problem,' Ellen assured her. 'Visitors rarely bring their own unless they're staying. There's enough spares to fit out an army.'

In the changing rooms, already deserted by the rest of the company, Sherry chose a bikini while Ellen flung off her fabulous gown as if it was a rag and flew to join them.

'Be seeing you,' she waved. 'No hurry.'

Sherry didn't hurry, because she was doubtful about the briefness of the bikini. The only three suits she could find were obviously miles too big, so she had to settle for what fitted. Nevertheless, she didn't care for feeling so naked.

Eventually she had to move. Distant splashing and laughter indicated there was more fun to be had than she was having standing here! Approaching the pool by the longest path, she gave a startled gasp on suddenly finding herself confronted by Scott. Having left him deep in conversation with Dulcie Easten, he was the last person she expected to see.

So quickly she could do nothing to prevent it, his arm shot out and she was drawn into the darker shade of the surrounding trees. There was little light. What there was seemed to be piercing her from his silvery eyes.

Trying not to appear too startled, she gulped and asked, 'Did you want something, Mr Brady?'

'An explanation, perhaps?'

It must be strange, when she could see nothing else, how clearly she saw his eyes narrowing, his black brows drawing together.

'I beg your pardon,' she whispered, keeping her voice low so he wouldn't detect it was trembling. 'I'm afraid I don't understand.'

His laughter was a low, mocking sound which she wished didn't sound so attractive to her ears. 'I think you do,' he said softly. 'This particular party was your idea, Miss Grant, and though I'm past the age for playing games, I agreed, albeit reluctantly, to go ahead with it.'

'S-so?'

'I don't like being made a fool of.'

'Would I ever be so ambitious?' Attempting to equal his mockery, she tilted her head to stare at him, but shied away as their eyes met and a thousand shattering shocks raced through her. In the shimmering light a million tensions were besetting her, in no way relieved by the harshness of his next words.

'I told you the other night, I refuse to make high drama out of this. Despite your traitorous little protests, you obviously have more liking for it than I have, but I assure you this evening won't be repeated.'

Bitterly she retorted, 'Was it very admirable to want to show Kim and me up?'

'That's beside the point,' he replied. 'It was you, yourself, who suggested it. All I'm interested in is holding two people back from what could be a monumental disaster. If this could have been achieved discreetly, well and good, but as it seems impossible, I won't waste any more time. From now on I shall forbid Ellen to see your brother, and I want your promise that you won't encourage Kim to go against my ruling.'

'Or else, Mr Brady?'

His teeth flashed, hard and white in the darkness. 'I must say, Sherry, I admire your intelligence. Go against me and you're in for the shock of your life. If anything happens to Ellen, I guarantee there'll be reprisals.'

When he used her name, all her senses heightened. His eyes held hers, very dark and challenging. She had to shake her head to get rid of the sensation that she was drowning. From a great distance she heard her own voice, amazingly light and disdainful. 'Threats, Mr Brady?'

His mouth thinned. 'At the moment, but not idle ones.'

Sherry tried to calm the strange buoyancy which was driving her on. She might have shared some of Kim's recklessness, for the desire to goad Scott Brady was irresistible. 'What could happen to Ellen?' she asked, deliberately provoking. 'Isn't a girl of twenty-four old enough to be responsible for her own destiny?'

'Do I have to keep repeating?' he said curtly. 'Ellen's led a very sheltered life. She could be seduced. In the hands of a fortune-hunter it could easily happen.'

Sherry went still, completely stunned by such bluntness. She ignored the small voice within her that said she had asked for it. 'Kim wouldn't!' she spluttered. 'And he's no fortune-hunter.'

'He acts like one,' Scott had no pity for her surprising paleness. 'And it's a mistake to pretend he's a saint.'

Sherry lost control of herself then, incited beyond endurance. 'Are you?' she cried ridiculously, raising small fists to begin hitting him.

He didn't flinch, she might merely have been patting

his broad chest. He caught hold of her, though, giving her a little shake. 'That's enough, Sherry.'

How could she ever listen to such a relentless voice, devilishly overtoned in velvet though it was! Never had she felt less like pulling herself together. Everything was getting too much, and pounding this impossible man might be the best way of releasing her pent-up fury. She forgot she was wearing practically nothing until he pulled her hard against him, his arms encircling her slight body, his hands biting in to her soft skin.

While she gasped, he taunted mockingly, 'You'd be a fool if you believed any man a saint, Sherry. This little exercise might prove it.'

He eased her slightly away, subjecting her to a cool, searching scrutiny. Helplessly, Sherry looked at him, her lips quivering, her wide blue eyes darkening in horrified anticipation. He couldn't be thinking of kissing her, could he? She had never meant to drive him that far! 'Don't dare touch me!' she breathed.

His enigmatical gaze was roaming her face, his voice cynical. 'You throw yourself at me, then ask me not to touch you. You imply I'm a scoundrel, the least you can expect is for me to kiss you.'

'No!' she cried numbly, only being able to appeal to him verbally, all physical strength having left her.

Derisively he drawled, 'Don't worry, I won't ask the supreme sacrifice. When I really want to make love to a girl, I pick one with more experience.'

He bent to touch her lips with his, clearly intent, from his sardonic expression, on frightening her more than anything else. There might have been no thought of his own satisfaction, otherwise. So why, after the first brief second, did the pressure of his mouth suddenly deepen and a shudder run through his tall frame?

Sherry felt boneless and quiescent, drugged to her extremities. She heard the harsh intake of his breath as his mouth forced hers open with ruthless precision. As his arms drew her closer, her own went fiercely round his neck. It was the first time any man had kissed her but she acted as if it had been happening for years. His hand shaped the back of her head, his technique so sensual she couldn't match it, but she began returning his kisses passionately, her fingers digging into his shoulders as she clung to him.

Just when her blood was beginning to take fire, he lifted his head abruptly. Every nerve end suddenly pulsing with awareness, she might have fallen if he hadn't continued holding her. After a moment, when she regained her balance, he thrust her nearly savagely from him.

His voice came rasping. 'Words are wasted on a girl like you!'

Brushing a tear from her eye, she hoped he didn't notice. 'What were you trying to prove?' she whispered, her mind shattered in chaos.

'Do I have to spell it out?' His dark face was once again formidable. 'I curtailed myself to a few kisses, but I'm sure you're quite able to imagine how much more difficult it might have been if we'd fancied ourselves in love.'

His tenaciousness was astounding! Kim and Ellen didn't stand a chance! She couldn't begin to analyse her own feelings, they were so complex she wouldn't dare examine them! With a choked cry, she turned and ran from him, but even as he let her go she doubted if she would ever escape the new emotions he had roused in her.

The following days became weeks and passed slowly. After the dinner party at Coomarlee, Kim had grown strangely secretive. Amazingly he took to following a more regular routine of work, going out early in the morning and frequently staying out all day. Old Sam and his son weren't saying much—but then they rarely did. Perhaps they were waiting to see if Kim's transformation was genuine before they lauded him with praise. If she didn't see a lot of Kim herself, it was because she worked nearer the homestead. Mustering the big Merinos was a tiring operation for a slip of a girl. By sundown she was exhausted and glad to return to the homestead to prepare the evening meal. Afterwards she usually went straight to bed.

Of Scott Brady she had seen no sign since the dinner-party. Having seen nothing of Ellen, either, she concluded Scott had carried out his threat and removed her to one of his other properties. She was sure Kim wasn't still seeing her. Since trying to get a few straight answers out of Kim about his relationship with Ellen, she hadn't broached the subject again. It wasn't easy to talk to him. She had to catch him in the right mood, and she was always busy.

She didn't know when she first noticed that Kim had lost weight and looked depressed. Believing he was settling down, it was a rude shock to suddenly realise he was brooding a lot. One evening she plucked up courage to ask what was wrong.

'Everything,' he replied cynically, 'and nothing.'

Sherry immediately felt apprehensive. 'Is it Ellen?'

'How did you guess?' he muttered sarcastically.

She looked at him doubtfully. 'I hadn't seen her round, I thought she might be away.'

Kim's eyes hardened as he returned his sister's gaze, but he was obviously seeing other than Sherry's tired face. 'Scott wanted her to go, but she refused, He watches her like a hawk, though. If he's not keeping an eye on her, he makes sure someone is.'

So Scott's threats hadn't been idle ones! Sherry frowned unhappily. How much of this had been her fault? She hadn't collaborated with Scott; if she had, ironically she might have been able to do more for Kim, indirectly, than she was able to do now. Yet mightn't a complete break be better, in the long run? She had to agree with Scott that Kim wasn't in the position to be thinking seriously of any girl.

Sherry felt it would be cruel to keep on telling him

that, and found herself weakly observing, 'He can't keep her prisoner!'

'No, but he can be damned awkward.'

She could imagine! She asked tentatively, 'When was the last time you were with her?'

Kim's hesitation was so slight as to be scarcely discernible. 'The night of the dinner party.'

Sherry recalled that night with flushed cheeks. How long had Scott and she been under those trees? Ten minutes or half an hour? She had refused to allow herself to dwell on such a humiliating episode! Whenever it impinged on her mind, she refused to think about it. Scott must have felt a similar aversion, for she had scarcely seen him again that evening. He had rejoined the company indoors while she had shakenly re-dressed and hidden in a quiet corner of the garden to contemplate her shame. Not until she gauged the swimming session over had she returned to join the younger ones on the terrace where they had danced to the music coming through the open windows.

So absorbed did she become in the sudden rush of recollections that she wasn't prepared for the shock that rushed through her as she heard Kim muttering bitterly, 'Sometimes I feel like doing something desperate!'

CHAPTER THREE

SHERRY visibly started as she was immediately besieged by memories of events even more disturbing than those she had been thinking of. As Kim spoke, all the doubts regarding their father's sudden death returned devastatingly. Flooded by barely controllable apprehension, she stared at her brother, despairing to see how pale he looked, and indeed desperate.

Sherry trembled like a wind-tossed leaf. It struck her suddenly that she must do something. She had been considering the whole affair mainly from Ellen's point of view, the apparent hopelessness of it, as pointed out by Scott Brady. But surely if Ellen's happiness depended on having a permanent relationship with Kim, Scott should be prepared to help him?

At Googon, Kim was like a square peg in a round hole, but his potential in the right place might be enormous. He had a lot of their father in him. Her small face set in lines of painful concentration, Sherry tried to recall instances almost forgotten, and her groping mind eventually pounced on something concrete: her father in conversation with one of his top men. Harold Gibson, entirely dependable and trustworthy, had always been a tower of strength. Though his own health had failed a few months before the crash, he had wanted Kim to stay in London and stick it out, sure that something could be salvaged. She had heard him remarking to her father that Kim showed great promise. No unparalleled recommendation, one might think, but no one knowing Harold Gibson would have failed to be impressed. If she could convey some of this to Scott Brady, mightn't he believe it would be worthwhile giving Kim a chance in one of his own companies? It might mean explaining something of what had happened in London, and after three years of silence that wouldn't be easy, but if it was for Kim's ultimate happiness she believed she could do it.

The question of Googon's possible fate, should Kim leave, she thrust to one side. She hadn't lived here for three years without learning that survival could depend on conserving her strength for the problems on hand, not those which might never happen. She only let herself conjecture that if Scott wanted Googon it might be an added incentive to transferring Kim to a job he liked, but she shied away, with the caution of someone twice her age, from imagining it was something already accomplished.

Not obviously eager to await any comments on his bitterness, Kim slammed out violently, leaving Sherry in a terrible state of indecision. Despite Harold Gibson's opinion of him, Kim's moods were often so unreliable that she hesitated to recommend him to anyone.

Advising herself to think carefully, she did nothing for the next few days, yet the sight of Kim's unhappy face became more than she could stand. Desperately she tried to think of another course of action, somewhere between Scott's ruthless one and her own perhaps too ambitious one. When one evening Kim came home from Bourke, in what could only be described as a drunken stupor, Sherry was driven to making up her mind. She had to make one last attempt to help Kim or somehow she would always believe she had failed him, as well as their parents.

Having put him to bed, with the help of old Sam, she took the truck and set out for Coomarlee. She didn't give a thought to the fact that she might arrive in the middle of dinner. She was so wholly concerned for Kim, the certain knowledge that he needed help, she didn't spare a thought for anything else.

On the way she collected a flat and had to change the

wheel. Fortunately the spare was all right, but as she parked outside Coomarlee's imposing front door, she glanced ruefully at her dirty hands. She had done her best with a rag, but hadn't been able to get rid of all the grease.

There were two other cars in the drive. Stopping near them, she had no means of knowing if they belonged to Scott. If he had guests he might be annoyed if she disturbed him, but she had no means of finding out. Brushing back her hair, which she had returned to its usual practical braid after being here last, she squared her thin shoulders and knocked on the door.

An elderly woman, presumably the housekeeper, answered.

'I'd like to see Mr Brady, please,' Sherry said.

The woman frowned. 'Mr Brady has guests.'

'I see.' Sherry didn't retreat—her mission was too important. That Scott was at home was too great an advantage to dismiss easily. 'I wonder if you could ask if he would spare me a little of his time?'

'I think,' the woman advised doubtfully, 'you'd better make an appointment to see him when it's more convenient, Miss——?'

'Grant,' Sherry supplied absently.

'Grant . . .!' The pair of brown eyes studied her a little more sharply. 'From—Googon?'

'Yes,' Sherry nodded as casually as she was able. 'It's a long way.'

It wasn't, and the woman didn't look impressed. Far from it! 'I'm afraid I have my orders,' she began.

Sherry wasn't listening. Beyond the housekeeper's sentinel shoulders, she saw the lounge door opening and Scott coming out, closing the door behind him. Glancing at the girl hovering on his doorstep, he might have been blind, for his feet never hesitated in the way he was going.

Incensed at being so ignored, Sherry acted on impulse. Angrily brushing past his housekeeper, she flew after him, catching his arm. 'Mr Brady!' she exclaimed. 'I'd like a word with you.'

He paused on a half turn, immediately detaching her less than clean fingers from the sleeve of his immaculate suit. His eyes, no less unfriendly than his housekeeper's, coldly surveyed her flushed face. 'Do you make a habit of invading a man's privacy, Miss Grant?'

Had she ever been held in this man's arms, kissed by him as though he enjoyed what he was doing? Glaring at him, she retorted, 'I asked to see you and was refused. It was the only way.'

'Really, Miss Grant,' he shamed her wildness by being derisively reasonable, 'you could have returned another day, if it was important. I have guests.'

'So she told me.'

Her perhaps less than reference to a member of his staff tightened his lips. 'Mrs Fox.'

'Well, she has that look. I didn't know her name!'

'Remember it, if you ever have the occasion to use it again.' His tone implied she wouldn't. 'Now, will you please get out of my sight!'

'No, I won't!' Sherry's incredulous gasp held a determination to stay right where she was until he listened. 'It's about Kim and Ellen,' she added quickly, as he seemed about to eject her by bodily force.

He paused, uncharacteristically uncertain, and Sherry had to press a momentary advantage. 'I have something to say, and you must listen!'

Again the odd hesitation, but if he was waging a battle it wasn't with herself. 'I don't have to listen to anything, Miss Grant.'

'I know!' she flung back her head despairingly. 'You never listen unless you want to. Perhaps that's where you go wrong, Mr Brady!'

If she had expected him to be annoyed, she wasn't prepared to find herself being thrust so forcibly into his study. As the door closed, he checked a gold watch on his hair-sprinkled wrist. 'I'll spare you five minutes, Miss Grant.'

Sherry stared at him, maybe a shade more anxiously now she had got her way. Five minutes! She didn't underestimate the command in the dark-timbred voice—it wouldn't be a minute longer. Sighing at her own foolishness, she wished she hadn't lost her temper. Anger wasn't easy to get rid of at the drop of a hat, and time was ticking away inexorably.

'It's about Kim . . .'

'And Ellen, you said,' Scott prompted impatiently as she hesitated.

'Yes. Yes, I did.' If only she could get on with it instead of reducing what time she had with inane observations. The trouble was her mind had gone blank! She tried again. 'Well, Kim has been so depressed lately, I had to come and see if you wouldn't relent. About letting Ellen see him, I mean.'

'He sent you?'

Did he have to sound so disparaging? If Kim had, would it have been a crime? 'He has no idea I'm here,' she said.

'Why not?'

Sherry stared at him, unconsciously mutinous. The way he was sniping at everything she said wasn't helping. 'We don't always tell each other where we're going.'

His mouth curled, reflecting the contemptuous look on his face. 'I saw him in Bourke, round five o'clock.'

'Oh.' Her glance wavered frustratedly. That said everything! Scott Brady would never want anyone who was indiscreet enough to get drunk on the streets for a brother-in-law.

'So,' he continued, with aggravating astuteness, 'after putting him to bed, you decided you couldn't put up with it any longer and raced over here.'

'I got a flat tyre,' she muttered distractedly.

'Which explains why you're covered in grease.'

She hadn't given it much thought, but he was looking so hard at her face, she realised there must be grease there too. Hastily she took a handkerchief from her pocket and began scrubbing her cheeks.

'Leave it!' he muttered tersely. 'It's only a smudge.'

She shrugged her shoulders but immediately obeyed. What difference would it make if she was spick and span and beautiful? He had made up his mind about the Grants and nothing she either said or did was going to change it! She ought to go straight home.

Yet she was loath to leave before making one last plea on Kim's behalf. Scott was watching her narrowly and she tried to be coolly rational. It might not be fair to expect him to be impressed when he knew so little of the real Kim.

'In the right place,' she said carefully, 'my brother could do well, Mr Brady. He has a degree and it was considered he had a brilliant future.'

'By whom?'

Was there no pity in the man's iron soul? Sherry had to gaze at the floor to hide a despairing indignation. 'Harold Gibson, my father's right-hand man . . .'

'Come again?'

Now he was openly mocking her. 'I'm aware you know nothing of my family history, Mr Brady.'

'I know your father was less than honest.'

'Who told you that?'

'Don't look so incensed. Your grandfather made it common knowledge.'

Naturally! Sherry felt more despair. Grandfather would have had to have some reason for turning his back on his daughter's husband, and his subsequent harsh treatment of her children. To pretend their father was a scoundrel would justify his attitude more convincingly than had it been known Richard Grant was a successful and honourable financier. If only she could have pleaded he had been to the end, what a difference it would have made. She would never believe her father had been less than straight, but others demanded proof.

She said, a little wildly because she felt so strongly about it, 'I'll never believe my father was less than honest. Misguided, perhaps . . .'

Pure derision lit Scott's grey eyes. 'Isn't it often the same thing?'

'Grandfather shouldn't have made such terrible accusations without proof, but he was an old man.'

Nothing masked the deepening contempt on Scott's face. 'Do you intend spending your life finding excuses for your family, Sherry? Your swindling father has been deceived, your old reprobate of a grandfather is to be forgiven because of his age, and your lazy brother has never had a chance. You have no proof that Kim is any better than he appears to be, and yet you want me to take him on.'

'Will you stop!' she protested violently. 'I might have been mistaken in coming to Coomarlee, but it was with the best of intentions, and I don't have to put up with your insults!' Her blue eyes blazed until Scott began staring into them, as if captivated against his will by their beauty. He remained silent as she rushed on. 'Ruthlessness might have got you where you are, Mr Brady, but don't you care who you trample on to keep your snug little world intact? You forget others don't always have your strength, but even the strong can be misled.' Curiously she thought of Dulcie Easten, lovely but scheming. 'You might be yourself!'

'Not if I keep my eyes open,' he retorted icily, 'and disregard plausible young women like yourself. I got where I am by hard work, Miss Grant. I don't know what line of business your father was in . . .?'

'He was a—financier.'

Noticing her slight hesitation, Scott's voice was sarcastic. 'Back-street money-lenders call themselves that.'

Infuriated, Sherry flew at him. She could stand only

so much, Dear God, she couldn't be expected to put up with everything! Her eyes were sparkling and she gasped with pain as he caught the hand she raised in anger.

Suddenly the atmosphere changed. It was so startling that her breath caught in her throat and her heart began beating rapidly. They were caught in the same high-tensioned spiral as they had been the last time she was here. Feeling trapped, she gazed at him helplessly.

His glance speared her, his fingers biting so cruelly into the arm he was holding, and she realised he wasn't entirely conscious of what he was doing. She was made dizzy by electrical sensations she seemed unable to control, and when his head bent as his mouth found hers, she was overwhelmed by the blackness of his eyes.

Locked in a vice-like hold, she was pressed against his hard body, experiencing the turmoil of a kiss that sent darts of flame through her. The sensation was incredible. In the moments he held her it mounted until her whole body was writhing and she could no longer contain it. As his mouth hardened and his arms crushed her closer so she couldn't scream, tears forced their way through her tightly closed lids.

The dampness of them against his face might have brought a measure of sanity to the man holding her, for with a harsh exclamation she was released. Without pausing to notice the dark colour under his skin, she stumbled blindly towards the door.

In the huge hallway she nearly crashed into a couple walking along it, an older man, a younger woman.

'Good heavens!' she heard the woman exclaim as she rushed past them. 'Isn't that that wretched girl from Googon? Scott, darling . . .'

Sherry heard no more as she ran to the truck, which thank goodness started up at the first attempt. She was grateful, too, that the drive was wide, because her steering wasn't too good to begin with. Her hands were shaking, she knew she would have to stop to give herself time to calm down. She didn't dare recall being in Scott's arms. When she did, her heart reacted violently, every nerve in her body tightening so excruciatingly she had to bite her lip to stop crying out. If she had ever thought about it, she would never have believed it was possible to be more frightened of her feelings than anything else. It dismayed her to realise she was more terrified of Scott Brady's kisses than anything else he might dish out.

She tried to be rational. Why should she feel so stirred up at being kissed? Perhaps because it hadn't happened to her often enough. It might make sense to go out with a few men and experiment. She wondered why she had absolutely no inclination to do so.

A few miles on she left the road, bringing the truck to a halt under the shelter of some gum trees. Still on Scott Brady's land, she noticed the difference between Coomarlee and Googon. When he was here, Scott was never off the job. She was aware of his contempt for lazy graziers, but he had both money and equipment. His light aircraft skimmed his paddocks trailing superphosphate which vastly improved the condition of the grazing, which was obviously advantageous in times of drought. He also used light aircraft to see where his sheep were during mustering, which made things a lot easier for his men. At Googon they couldn't afford a decent truck, let alone anything else!

Resting her face against the steering wheel, Sherry wasn't conscious of the tears still pouring down her cheeks until they began falling on her hands.

'Mission not accomplished!' she sniffed on an uneven breath, talking to herself raggedly, as she had a habit of doing in times of stress. Quickly she brushed the tears from her eyes. It didn't do to weep over every failure. She had rarely wept since her parents died, not since Kim had shaken her and said tears accomplished nothing. He had been just as upset, if in a different way. His grief had been the bitter, resentful kind.

Next morning Kim looked dreadful, and she didn't dare mention what a mess she had made of things. Her visit to Coomarlee would have to remain a secret, but that didn't settle her conscience. Scott's opinion of them would be worse than ever, which must be her fault. As she dosed Kim with a powerful cure for a hangover, passed on by an old Aborigine, she felt as despairing as he clearly did.

Eventually Kim said he felt better, and she almost believed him when he surprised her by suggesting that they had a night out in Bourke, the following evening.

'A—night out?' They were having coffee after dinner, a second cup, after the men had gone, and she glanced at him, startled. 'What sort of a night out?'

Kim shrugged. 'Oh, nothing sensational. Just a meal and a few drinks with friends.'

'Which friends?'

He laughed. 'Don't look so suspicious, honey! It suddenly struck me how little fun you've had in your life. You hardly know anyone of your own age, but what happens when I try and do something about it? My good intentions are immediately suspect.'

'You know it's not that!' Sherry said lamely. 'If we hadn't been so busy lately, I might have jumped at the chance.'

'We have been busier,' he replied impatiently, and, as she still hesitated, 'Well, how about it?'

'If you like,' she knew she must seem annoyingly unenthusiastic, but she had never felt less like going anywhere. Hopefully she tried the excuse she had used when she had been trying to wriggle out of going to Coomarlee. 'What about a dress, though? You know I haven't anything very suitable to go out in.'

'You looked good enough when we dined at Coomarlee,' he retorted, 'so don't let that put you off.'

As Kim was apparently determined to take her out, she gave in. She made herself think that an evening away from Googon might do her good.

They were mustering near their boundary with Coomarlee the following afternoon, when Sherry saw Scott Brady and two other men approaching. Her cheeks flushed, despite herself, as they halted within a few yards of the poor-looking bunch of sheep she and Sam had rounded up. As Sam doffed his hat—too respectfully, she thought sourly—Scott spoke to her.

'Good morning, Miss Grant.'

His grey eyes were impossible to read. 'Good morning,' she returned stiffly, determined to be polite.

The other men looked at her curiously, one very curiously indeed, as if something about the delicate structure of the girl on the white horse captivated his imagination. He kept glancing at Scott. He couldn't have made it clearer that he was waiting to be introduced.

Scott and Sherry stared at each other for several seconds before he obliged. 'Miss Grant,' he drawled, still without moving his eyes from her face, 'Barry White, from Sanca Downs.'

He didn't mention the second man, but as he was also a stranger she presumed he must be on the staff of Sanca Downs. Sherry noticed Scott didn't say where she was from, and her soft mouth tightened as she wrenched her eyes from him to smile at Barry White.

'Hello,' she said.

Barry's brows shot up at her clear English voice, its gentle tones reminding him of greener places. 'Hello,' he replied, holding out his big hand, his face creased in a big smile. 'I realise I live in another territory, but how come this is the first time we've met?'

'Miss Grant keeps busy,' Scott interposed dryly.

'Hasn't Miss Grant got a name?' Barry exclaimed, then flushed with what looked like unusual embarrassment while Scott frowned.

'It's Sherry,' Sherry said hastily, tightening her grip on her reins in an attempt to stop her heart racing. If she had gained an unexpected admirer in Barry White, who appeared young and very personable, it was Scott Brady who could upset her equilibrium at a glance. He looked so magnificent on his huge black stallion, she began to feel the same symptoms which had so frightened her the last time she had seen him. Ostensibly, to hide this, she smiled at Barry more warmly than she might otherwise have done and he responded very warmly indeed.

'You live at Googon?' Barry's query proved that though he might not live here, he was no stranger to the district.

'My brother owns it.' Sherry didn't add that it was mortgaged up to the hilt.

Barry proceeded eagerly, 'I'd be interested to see over your property some time, Miss Sherry. Those sheep of yours look just fine!'

She knew it wasn't true. The state of the stock on Googon, ravaged by lack of attention and drought, was less than good. She envied Scott his better irrigation, the facilities he had, such as being able to remove his stock to other areas when things got really bad. She didn't need to glance at him to see his reaction to Barry's remark. Barry's voice might lack the conviction of his words, but she chose only to hear the kindness in it and to see the genuine liking in his eyes.

She chose also to defy a sense of caution. Never had she felt more reckless. 'I'm usually busy, Barry, as Mr Brady pointed out, but I'm sure if you give us a ring some time, my brother would like to show you round.'

'That really is very good of you!' Barry—it might have been a case of love at first sight—wasn't disguising the fact that he intended taking up her offer the first chance he got. 'I wonder...?' He paused, so clearly considering how he could make this sooner, rather than later that he might have spoken aloud.

'Another time, perhaps,' Scott broke in coolly. 'Now, gentlemen, if I could have a quick word with Miss Grant?'

Noticeably puzzled by such formality, Barry nodded to his foreman and moved on. 'I'll be in touch. Good day to you, Miss Sherry.'

If such deference appeared to annoy Scott, he didn't remark on it. Sherry thought perhaps he had developed the habit of tightening his lips when she was around. Compulsively her eyes stayed on him, rather than Barry's retreating figure, and she shivered.

'Cold, Miss Sherry?'

'No,' she flushed at his derision.

'I shouldn't encourage Barry, if I were you,' he advised, causing Sherry to exclaim heatedly, 'What is this? First you're warning Kim to stay away from your sister, now I'm to stay away from Barry White! If it gratifies you, I have no particular wish to start a beautiful friendship with Mr White.'

'Why ask him to Googon, then?'

She gazed at him frustratedly, nibbling her full bottom lip with small white teeth. Why did Scott ask when he sounded so uninterested? 'I had no desire to be impolite . . .'

'You feel no such compunction towards me?' he cut in sarcastically.

'Do you think you deserve it?' she asked, mutinous feelings written all over her face.

'There's no need to hate me,' he said coldly, 'because I make a few honest remarks about your brother.'

Sherry went rigid with stupefaction. 'I didn't escape entirely.'

'I have nothing against you personally, Sherry.'

'You could have fooled me!' she retorted, uncaringly defiant, colour eddying under her fine skin.

He studied her narrowly, sitting so easily on his evil-eyed mount, which might have thrown a lesser man. Sherry was stunned by his vitality, the explosive, dangerous quality she sensed in him. She found it difficult to keep her eyes off the picture they made, he and his horse. Horses recognised strength but only accepted it if it was the right kind. Obviously this horse had something of the devil in him and responded to Scott as a kindred spirit. Scott would be good at controlling both horses and women. He must find it frustrating that his young neighbour was proving to be the exception.

Because she wasn't as sure of that as she would liked to have been, she moved under his surveillance uneasily, hoping it wasn't to be an open contest of wills. She was vaguely glad of Sam's distant but comforting presence. She had no idea what Scott wanted to speak to her about, but Sam constituted a form of protection she wouldn't be without.

Scott broke the unnerving silence. 'To prove my point, Miss Grant'—why had she the feeling it was one of the few times in his life he had bothered trying to prove anything to someone like herself—'I'm going to invite you to join me for dinner, this evening. I'll call for you at seven.'

'Oh!' Her lips parted in sheer astonishment and her eyelids fell. It was the last thing she had expected. Certainly she wasn't prepared for it. Had fate been protecting her by prompting Kim to ask her out first? Forcing herself to look at him again, she breathed nervously, 'I'm sorry, Mr Brady, I'm afraid I have a prior engagement.'

Echoes of her mother! How often had she heard her murmuring that, if with much more aplomb, to someone over the telephone. Occasionally it seemed to Sherry that some part of her mother's personality still influenced her.

'Another engagement?' Her thoughts were abruptly interrupted by Scott's open disbelief.

Sherry sensed a storm brewing. It hadn't broken, but there was a danger it might. The colour in her cheeks became a rosy flush as her temper heightened defensively to meet it. 'You sound as if you think it impossible!'

He countered silkily. 'It seems a remarkable coincidence.'

She had to allow that it could seem like that, but she was too angry at his unspoken implications to be reasonable. So he thought no one else would ever ask her out! Well, let him! 'That's life,' she muttered, glaring at him.

'I'd like to slap that expression off your face,' he said grimly. 'You must have been a spoiled child.'

'No, Mr Brady,' for a moment her blue eyes were bleak, 'I certainly wasn't.'

'Self-pity, Miss Grant?'

She shook her head a little wildly so that her hat was dislodged. He caught it as it slipped sideways, clamping it back on her head. 'How you keep that rose-petal complexion beats me,' he said derisively, his hand slipping to her shoulder.

Their eyes met and locked with the now familiar intensity while their breath intermingled audibly. Sherry's heart threatened to fail her if he didn't let go, yet she couldn't lift a finger to assist her own release. She felt she was drifting like a leaf towards a fiercely flowing river, helpless to prevent her own destruction.

'Who's taking you out this evening?' he asked abruptly, the hand on her shoulder like a vice.

It would have been a simple matter to tell him, but too humiliating. He would only laugh, he might even bully her—the word blackmail also went through her mind—into cancelling her dinner with Kim. Well, Kim probably needed her company more than he did, and although Scott had asked her out with seemingly good intentions, she didn't for one moment believe he would be devastated by her refusal.

'I'd rather not say,' she replied coldly.

'As you wish.' He gave her a long, level look as his hands returned to his reins and he wheeled his horse to follow his friends. 'Maybe another time, Miss Grant.'

Sherry watched him riding away until she became

aware of Sam watching her and with a self-conscious flush went back to her work. There was plenty to do, but she didn't complain. Suddenly, as Scott's abrupt departure left a chill in her heart, her work here became doubly precious.

As she and Sam slowly drove the reluctant sheep towards the homestead, besieged in the heat by determined flies, her thoughts became increasingly troubled. After three years she had begun taking Googon for granted, imagining it would always be there. Suddenly, as the trauma of their recent misfortunes hit her, she knew it might not be there much longer. Eventually Kim might be forced to sell, and what then? The future was something she rarely allowed herself to contemplate, as she was doing now. The meagre sum Kim might have left after the mortgage and other debts had been settled might be only enough to take them back to the city. Then what? she asked herself again. A small flat, if they were fortunate enough to find one, in a district they could afford? And neither Kim or she trained for anything. A dry sob escaped Sherry's throat, forcing her to think of other things.

She wondered why Scott had asked her out. She couldn't really believe the reason he had given, she was sure it hadn't been on sudden impulse, yet she couldn't come up with anything else. He had said he wanted to speak to her about something, but whatever it was it couldn't have been important, because he hadn't mentioned anything. Perhaps he had merely been trying to save his friend from her less than desirable clutches. Sherry's lips twisted humourlessly.

She couldn't blame Scott for being so unflatteringly doubtful that she already had a date, but she was glad she did have a valid reason for not accepting his invitation. It didn't occur to her until she was hurrying to change, that evening, that he might have wanted to talk to her again about Ellen and Kim. It distressed her to realise that, through a lack of foresight, she might have missed a chance that might never come again, but she had no time to dwell on it.

She discarded her blue dress in favour of her other one, a deep pink which made her skin look like a wild rose. Scott's comment made her notice her skin as she hadn't done before. While studying her reflection, she was surprised to note how little fashions had altered in the past three years. The dress was calf-length, the same length that Princess Diana so often favoured. Sherry thought wistfully that she would love to see Princess Diana when she came here on tour, but she didn't suppose she would get the chance.

The pink dress was very well cut and she remembered it had been expensive. Hesitantly she took from her drawer a heavy gold locket and chain she had been given by her parents. The colours of the enamel toned with her dress perfectly and she brushed aside a surge of sadness.

'That's new,' Kim frowned, as she went to find him.

Sherry glanced at him wryly. 'Before you begin lecturing me on extravagance, no, it isn't.'

If anything, Kim's frown deepened. 'If you had it, why didn't you wear it when we dined at Coomarlee?'

'I forgot about it. No, I didn't,' Sherry corrected herself, 'I'd forgotten it was a model. I just grabbed my blue one and didn't even look at it.'

'Pity,' he shrugged. 'If you'd worn that, you might have charmed Mr Brady more than you obviously did.'

She sighed, glancing away from him. 'Can't we forget Mr Brady for one evening?'

'Suits me,' he agreed curtly.

'Whereabouts are we going?' she asked as they set out. It might have been better to wait and see. If it was one of the best places she would worry over the cost. If it was just any old bar, she would worry about the company. Kim though had sunk into a morose mood after mentioning the Bradys, and, if she didn't believe it was her fault, she felt she must speak of something which might cheer him up.

'Bourke.' Briefly he named one of the best hotels.

Sherry could have kicked herself when she heard herself asking, 'Are you sure we can afford it?'

Kim laughed, appearing amused at last. 'If you got nothing else from the old man, at least you inherited his carefulness!'

She wasn't quick enough to hide the hurt in her eyes, and Kim's jeering glance was immediately apologetic.

'Sorry, honey,' he exclaimed, 'I didn't honestly mean to be nasty. And I promise, if I'm ever able to, I'll see you get your share. Grandfather didn't leave you anything, but you're really better out of it. At least if you don't have anything you can't be liable for anything.'

That was one way of looking at it. Sherry nodded, biting her lip. There was plenty she could say—not about how little she had, but of how little Kim was making of what he had! If he appeared to have settled down lately, she hoped it wasn't just a flash in the pan. Her glance wandered over the sulky lines of Kim's face and she wondered why she couldn't feel more optimistic.

CHAPTER FOUR

THE truck wasn't that comfortable and Sherry suffered from considerable jolting before they reached Bourke. It wasn't the roads so much as Kim's driving. He liked speed. Unfortunately the truck wasn't built for it and had seen better days.

After his first brief spate of conversation, Kim lapsed into silence again, making Sherry wonder what kind of an evening they were going to have. This was one of the few times she had been out with her brother since they had come to Australia. During school holidays, in England, she had sometimes tagged after him, but he had only allowed this during the daytime; the evenings he had spent with his friends. This evening he appeared to have a lot on his mind, and Sherry suddenly wondered if there wasn't more behind this outing than was immediately apparent. Why did she have an awful feeling that she was being made use of in some way?

Kim's mood was so tense she found herself considering each sentence before she spoke. One wrong word might be like a match to dynamite! What would he say, for instance, if she were to mention Scott had asked her out as well? No, she daren't risk it. Frowning, she studied her hands. How would she have been feeling if she'd been travelling to Bourke in Scott's company, with the prospect of spending several hours alone with him? He was probably relieved she had refused what she was certain must have been an invitation issued impulsively and as swiftly regretted. Even for his friends' sake, he couldn't have really meant to ask her out, not after the way he had treated her the last time she had been to Coomarlee!

Cautiously she decided against mentioning Scott's

invitation, but she did tell Kim about meeting him and Barry White. He could easily hear of this from another source and be angry that she had kept it from him.

When she finished speaking, Kim glanced at her sharply but merely said, 'You do get round.'

She persevered, ignoring the slight sarcasm in his voice, 'Do you know Mr White——'

'I know him by sight and reputation. He buys a lot of Brady's stud stock and it's rumoured he's nearly as wealthy.'

'He seems nice.'

'Did he have much to say?'

'Just that he would like to see over Googon some time.'

Emitting a low whistle, Kim exclaimed, 'Well, what do you know!' Mockingly he glanced at Sherry's startled face. 'You could do worse.'

She stared at him in confusion. 'I don't follow . . .'

Kim grinned. 'You don't think he's interested in either Googon or me?'

Unable to credit what he was implying, she countered coldly, 'Scott Brady's interested in Googon, at least we think he is.'

'Only because it adjoins his own land and would be useful.'

'You don't always have to want to buy something to be interested in it,' she argued.

Kim merely continued to grin, then asked suddenly, 'Where was Scott when all this was going on?'

Sherry's cheeks coloured vividly. 'There was nothing going on! You're the very limit, Kim, I wish I'd never told you! Scott was there.'

'If he thought White had taken a shine to you, he wouldn't be pleased, I bet!'

Sherry gasped, 'You aren't suggesting Scott could be jealous?'

Kim glanced at her impatiently. 'Not that way, you silly child! Don't you realise, Barry White's the man he's hoping Ellen will marry?'

If you waited long enough, there was usually an answer to everything. In this case it had come sooner than she might have expected. So Scott had asked her out to ensure she didn't steal Barry White from his sister, thus leaving the field clear for Kim.

'If what you say is true,' she said carefully, 'where was Mr White the night we went to Coomarlee?' In England it could be easy to say he lived too far away, but in this country people thought nothing of travelling a hundred miles to dinner, by road, and reducing such distances to nothing by plane.

'I don't know, do I?' Kim shrugged. 'The whole of that dinner-party was a mystery, but at least you're in the picture.'

'Would it help if I encouraged Mr White?' she asked slowly. She had no desire to, but she did feel sorry for Ellen and Kim.

'No,' mumbled Kim, adding on a lower note she was scarcely able to catch, 'Anyway, it's far too late.'

Sherry sighed. Whatever Kim meant, he sounded very despondent. She wished Scott had been here so she could have told him exactly what she thought of him. As for Ellen, if she hadn't the courage to hold out for the man she loved—well, she deserved to lose him!

Poor Kim! Gently, attempting to convey sympathy, she touched his arm as they stopped in front of the hotel.

'Here we are,' he said gruffly.

Was he embarrassed by her silent gesture? Glancing at him quickly, she saw his cheeks were tinged with red. Instinctively she thought of his heightened colour as guilt, then dismissed the idea as ridiculous.

As she scrambled out, he shrugged and turned away, leaving her to follow. It wasn't far to the entrance but suddenly she wished she had an escort who helped rather than ignored her, as some of the women had whom she noticed going in.

Inside, Kim did wait to guide her to the dining-room.

'It's late,' he said. 'I think we'd better eat straight away. We can have drinks at the table.'

The dining-room was large, with part of the floor left clear for dancing. The tables were grouped in a horseshoe around it, with a raised platform for a band at the other end. Sherry was amazed by the smartness of the décor, the general appearance of luxury emanating from the room. Bourke was an up-and-coming town, but she had never dreamt of anything like this!

'Impressed?' grinned Kim, as they were shown to one of the most prominent tables.

'Very,' she smiled back at him, determined not to be a wet blanket. She would have preferred to sit in a less obvious position, but Kim had no such inhibitions. He had never been as retiring as she was. He always enjoyed the limelight.

The lighting wasn't bright, but she had had the hazy impression, as they entered, that the restaurant was full. 'It's more like a nightclub,' she said, furtively looking round.

'The Aussie equivalent,' he nodded, 'but you'd be hard put to it to find better in London.'

She thought he was exaggerating a little but merely said. 'You still miss London?'

'What do you think!' he sighed. 'I'll always miss London.'

Sherry looked at the menu, ashamed to find herself studying the prices before the dishes. Frugality must have eaten its way into her very soul when she couldn't enjoy one evening out without worrying about the cost! Deliberately she chose the most expensive items, so that even Kim's brows went up. He didn't seem unusually disturbed, however, and ordered a rare vintage wine with another to accompany the main course.

'It's all on the house,' he murmured sotto voce, ignoring Sherry's enquiring brows.

She was still half frowning as the entree arrived. If

she'd asked Kim to explain even half of his ambiguous murmurings during the past weeks, she would have had no time left for anything else.

Because when she tried looking at other people, there seemed to be someone looking at her, she kept her eyes on either Kim or their table. She failed to see the tall man approaching and nearly choked on an oyster to find Scott Brady standing beside them. Eyes watering, she coughed, thinking Kim might have warned her!

'Good evening,' said Scott, his glance roaming in smouldering appraisal over Sherry's smooth dark hair, her small, distinctively striking features, sapphire blue eyes, sensuously curved mouth and firmly moulded chin.

'G-Good evening,' she stammered, while Kim nodded.

Scott was an entirely formidable figure, more so when he appeared both speculative and disapproving. At the moment he looked both as his eyes flicked narrowly from Sherry to the expensive repast on the table.

'Hoping to come into money?' he drawled at Kim.

If Kim hadn't flushed, Sherry mightn't have said anything. Scott, for some reason, was furious, though no one merely glancing at him could have detected it. 'We don't have to put up with your insults, Mr Brady!' she snapped.

'So you're always telling me,' he retorted sardonically, 'But I can't believe I'm always wrong.'

Without another word he left them. Sherry gazed with hatred at his broad, departing back.

'You surely wouldn't want him for a brother-in-law!' she exclaimed, more audibly than she realised, before she could stop herself.

Kim cocked an eyebrow, seemingly not half as disturbed as she was. 'It's a difficult enough job choosing a wife,' he shrugged. 'I think you have to accept her relations for better or worse.'

'Who is he with?' Agitatedly she remembered to lower her voice. Her evening was spoiled anyway. 'Oh, no!' Watching Scott until he reached his table, she noted several people who were strangers to her—and his sister, Ellen.

'Was this all arranged?' she accused Kim, looking at him bitterly.

His face closed up with its most secretive expression, so she knew she'd be lucky to be told the truth. 'Ellen did say she might be dining out,' he replied stiffly.

Sherry was so upset it didn't occur to her that he had practically confessed that he and Ellen had been in touch. 'She didn't say where?'

'I know she comes here,' he muttered evasively.

Sherry gazed blankly down at the congealed food on her plate. Only that afternoon, Scott had asked her to dine with him. He had given no indication that they would be joining anyone. Yet Kim, she realised intuitively, had known Ellen was going to be here yesterday, before he had issued an invitation to his sister. Sherry gave up; it was too complicated. She needed time to work it out.

'We'll have to leave as soon as we've finished eating,' she said sharply.

'Sure,' Kim agreed easily, but he didn't hurry.

Scott Brady's table was almost directly opposite. Sherry couldn't understand how she hadn't noticed him as soon as she came in. Clearly he and his guests were well through their meal. The way the waiters were hovering, for one thing, might have alerted her. Scott Brady was obviously a man who commanded the best attention!

Wishing Kim would get a move on, she quickly finished her dessert. From the corner of her eye she saw Ellen get to her feet with a tall young man. Lightly clasping, they joined the other couples on the floor. The music was dreamy. Sherry expected to see Kim's face darken with jealousy, but he didn't appear to be taking any notice, just went on steadily drinking.

Ellen, as her brother had done, paused beside their table. 'Hello,' she smiled. 'Excuse me butting in, but Ken here is dying to meet you, Sherry.'

A minute later, so quickly she wondered how it had happened, Sherry found herself introduced to Ken Frazer and sitting with him watching Ellen and Kim dancing. How it came about, Sherry wasn't sure, and frightened of Scott's reactions, she trembled apprehensively.

She didn't have long to wait before he came striding over, his face as black as the pants he was wearing. Ruthlessly taking hold of her, he pulled her into his arms. Ignoring a bewildered Ken, he snapped, 'Dance this with me.'

'I . . .' She began struggling, protesting wildly, when her eyes locked with his and she was helpless to withstand him. As she looked up at him and her senses reeled, she tried to blink, but found it impossible until another couple bumped into them, breaking the contact.

'You didn't say you were dining with your brother,' he said between his teeth, his eyes as hot as hers were behind their long lashes.

'You didn't give me a chance.'

'I suppose this was prearranged,' he retorted.

As this was exactly what she suspected herself, she had to deny it. 'I hardly think so. And,' she rushed on, despite being breathless, 'what about you? You didn't mention that you were asking me to join a party.'

'It wasn't going to be a party until an hour or two ago,' he said curtly. 'Some friends of Ellen's invited her here and I had to bring her.'

'Had to, Mr Brady?'

'No, damn you,' he snapped harshly, 'but I wasn't turning her loose at this stage.'

'I wonder you're allowing them to dance!' She glanced pityingly at Kim and his sister.

His voice held icy cruelty. 'That's all I am allowing, Miss Grant.'

His hands were digging into her flesh. Inside she began feeling she was on fire. She wondered if he was conscious of how much he was hurting her. Somehow she managed to force herself to concentrate on Ellen and Kim, to put their needs before her own.

'Isn't Mr White here?' she asked, she hoped coolly.

Scott tightened his grasp until his taut thighs were clamped against hers and she gasped at his audacity. 'No, Mr White is not!' he replied coldly.

Sherry tried to put a little distance between them but only succeeded in arousing his anger.

'Don't struggle,' he muttered, staring at her.

Sherry was too shaken to take any more evasive action. She had to go on speaking, even as the race of her heart grew so rapid she scarcely knew what she was saying. 'I believe you want Mr White for your sister, Mr Brady?'

He ignored this. 'No one appears to want my sister after they've seen you, Miss Grant. You bewitch men with your innocent blue eyes.'

The wine she had consumed must have affected her adversely, for to her horror she heard herself taunting, 'Surely not you, Mr Brady?'

His long hand slipped up her back, over her shoulders, curving round her nape, pressing her head under his chin. 'I might make love to you,' he murmured in her shell-like ear, 'but I'd never take you seriously. I allow myself to be bewitched by a woman only up to a certain point.'

'I thought you'd already been captivated by Miss Easten?' Sherry retorted shakily.

'Miss Easten's the kind of woman one marries,' he shrugged. 'You're not.'

'I may be poor,' she whispered furiously against his chest, 'but I'm not the other things you imply.'

'You will be,' he drawled. 'It might be sooner than you think if you don't stop playing with fire. I've told you before, it could be dangerous to involve yourself in your brother's schemes.'

His mouth grazed her ear before leaving it, making her pulse quicken in dizzy reaction. 'I haven't been involved in anything!' she gasped.

'Only a little double-dealing,' he countered. 'We all know what happens to spies who do that! I won't warn you again,' he said tightly. 'For the last time I'll repeat: if your brother ruins my sister's life, I'll do my best to ruin yours!'

Scott's threats were still affecting Sherry the next day. She trembled each time they crossed her mind. The evening, after a bad start, had had an even worse ending. While she danced with Scott, Kim and Ellen had disappeared outside and Scott had dragged her in pursuit of them. Sherry thought Kim should have known better than to act so recklessly right under Scott's nose, and with Scott at his heels she was despairing that he had allowed himself to be caught with Ellen in his arms.

It struck her that there was something odd about their embrace, but she had had no time to really consider it as Scott had torn the unfortunate couple apart. He hadn't been in the mood to look for anything suspicious. He had merely informed Ellen harshly that he was taking her home.

Kim and Sherry had left immediately as well, but on the journey back to Googon, whenever she had tried to say something, Kim had told her sharply to shut up.

After breakfast she went out with Sam and Jamie, leaving Kim to follow. It wasn't until around five in the afternoon that she began to be conscious of feeling uneasy. The temperature was high, but she was ashamed when she sometimes almost fell asleep in her saddle. She blamed the heat and being out so late the night before for making her so drowsy, otherwise she was sure she would have sensed sooner that something was wrong.

There had been no sign of Kim all day. This in itself

was no cause for alarm. Not infrequently, he took himself off to work alone at the other end of the station. When he didn't turn up for dinner, though, Sherry began getting anxious.

'I'll go and see what's keeping him, Sherry,' Jamie said, as she expressed concern. 'I'll take the bike.'

As he roared off, she blessed the kindness of the Googon men. For the most part they were silent and seemingly slow-moving, but no one coped with an emergency as they did. After coming here, Sherry had soon discovered it was amazing the amount of work these big silent men got through, and how really fast they could move when it was necessary.

Kim was nowhere to be found, but Sam advised Sherry not to worry. 'He could be anywhere,' he told her.

She went to look in his room and found a note. She opened it, vexed that she had missed it before when she had just glanced through the door.

'Sherry,' it read, 'I don't know how long I'll be away. Take care and don't worry.'

She showed it to Sam, because she had to tell someone. 'I can't understand,' she watched worriedly for his reactions. 'What do you think?'

'Beats me, Miss Sherry,' he frowned. 'He couldn't have eloped or something?'

Sam was joking, of course. It must be a joke to suggest Kim eloping! Or was it? Suddenly Sherry felt terribly shaken and knew she had to ring Coomarlee. She had to be convinced Kim would never commit such a folly as running off with Ellen Brady.

Helplessly she stared at Sam, Sam was getting on, but he had been with her grandfather all his life. His wife, Kathleen, had died young. Her grave lay on a hill behind the house, marked by a stone. He had been John Carey's overseer for years and during the old man's last illness, though Kim liked to pretend he had done it, it was Sam who had ran the station. He was a friend as well as a valued employee, and Sherry saw no reason why she shouldn't confide in him.

'I—I'm frightened he's gone off with Ellen Brady, Sam. He wouldn't do such a thing, would he?'

Sam glanced at her sharply. 'God help him if he has—her brother will skin him alive.'

Sherry shivered. 'That's what I'm afraid of!'

'All the same,' Sam muttered, his eyes shrewd and not unkind as they rested on her pale face, 'if it's help you're after, Scott Brady's the man to give it.'

Sherry didn't want to hear the respect in Sam's voice. Regard in these parts was never lightly earned or given, and she would much rather think of Scott as a villain. It almost hurt to admit reluctantly, 'It might be sensible to ring him.'

'I'm sure it would be,' Sam nodded wisely. 'Better being safe than sorry. If Ellen's there, at least you won't have to worry so much about Kim.'

Sam had scarcely finished speaking when the phone rang. Sherry hurried to pick it up. 'Sherry Grant...' she said breathlessly.

It was Scott Brady, but he didn't bother to introduce himself as Sherry had done. 'Is Ellen there?' he snapped.

It was the note of fury in his voice that flung her into panic. That, and the information gathered from his query that Ellen, like Kim, was missing. 'Ellen...?' she faltered weakly.

'You heard!' he rapped. 'Quit stalling, Sherry.'

She hadn't been—deliberately, but naturally he would think so! Dear God, where were her wits? 'No, she's not here.'

'Kim?' he barked next.

'K-Kim?'

'If you keep on repeating everything after me, Sherry,' the incensed voice advised, 'I'll beat you the next time I see you, and that's a promise!'

Still she prevaricated, despite being frozen with

fright. If she confessed that Kim wasn't here, he might believe he and Ellen were together. 'Maybe Ellen's just gone for a ride?' she faltered.

'Now why didn't I think of that?' he asked silkily, and rang off.

Half an hour later, as Sherry was still pondering uneasily on his last words, Scott flew in, in a light plane. He landed on the station runway, little used these days, and his long legs soon covered the short distance to the house. Someone should have fetched him, but the truck was gone.

His hard grey eyes swiftly assessed the small group watching his approach. 'I'd like a word with you, alone,' he said to Sherry, after nodding to the two men.

His hand was at her back as they went inside, she could feel the leashed anger in it. In the living-room he grasped her arm, swinging her round. 'Now,' he said savagely, 'I'd like an answer to my question. Where is he?'

This time Sherry had more sense than to be evasive. 'I don't know,' she replied unsteadily. 'I wish I did.'

'How long has he been missing?'

She wished he'd say Kim! 'The men and I have been out all day,' she told him. 'Kim was here when we left. We thought he might be at the other end of the run.'

'He isn't?'

'No. Jamie's been all over.'

Sherry swallowed. She was reluctant to tell him about Kim's note, but she thought she might have to. 'I thought you were watching her?'

'Unfortunately,' he replied icily, 'I didn't allow for her cunning—or maybe your brother's powers of persuasion. When we got in last night, she said she was very tired and would sleep late.' His eyes glittered briefly with self-derision. 'I believe I suggested it myself. Anyway, I conveyed the message to Mrs Fox, this morning, before I left for Broken Hill, where I had an appointment, that she wasn't to be disturbed. When I returned I found she had disappeared. The staff had been trying to get in touch with me since lunchtime, when it was discovered she was missing. I've been informed she was picked up by a light aircraft between twelve and one.'

Sherry was stunned. 'Kim just has the truck!'

Scott said flatly, 'I worked that out too. He hired a plane in Bourke. It's all too obvious they've gone off together.'

'You can't be sure!'

'When you pray,' he said sarcastically, 'get down on your knees, but I warn you, this time your prayers won't be answered. Read this.'

He thrust a note in her hands and she gazed at it in horror. It was like the one she'd received from Kim. She recognised Ellen's handwriting as her eyes skimmed the swiftly formed scrawl. She elaborated a little more than Kim, but not much.

'I'm going to be married, Scott,' she wrote. 'No matter how hard you try it's going to be too late to stop me. I hope, later, we can all be friends, you, my husband and I . . .'

As the piece of paper fluttered from Sherry's nerveless fingers, a funny little sound escaped her. 'Well!' she found herself laughing, her voice high with amusement, 'that seems to be that!'

Steely fingers contacted her cheek and she reeled at the slap she received. Never had she seen such cold fury in a man's face. As she swallowed painfully, Sherry's rising hysteria disappeared like water gurgling down a drain.

Without apology, he snapped, 'That isn't going to be that, as you so confidently put it, Miss Grant! We're going to find them.'

'We?' Brilliant blue eyes looked blankly at him from a white face.

'The two of us, Miss Sherry Grant.' His grey eyes

bored savagely into her. 'I think I might kill you for the help you've given them, but not before you've helped me find them.'

'I only tried——' she began.

'Spare me!' he snapped viciously. 'All you ever tried to do was improve your standard of living. An admirable ambition, if you and Kim hadn't decided to do it through Ellen. Well, whatever plans you made to cash in on my money, it's not going to pay off. Even if it takes days, I'll find your brother and Ellen and bring them back. I'll give you five minutes to get ready.'

Sherry could never recall being in quite such a state of turmoil as she was as she stumbled to do Scott's bidding. Her mind almost blanked out as she hurried to her room to find her purse. She had changed into a clean pair of cotton slacks before dinner and she left them on. They didn't stand on ceremony here as they did at Coomarlee. She wouldn't have dared wear them for dinner there! Or at home, in London, for that matter. Her mind unnaturally engaged with things that couldn't possibly be important at the moment, she returned to Scott.

She had never flown in a small plane. Her grandfather hadn't believed in them, the only concession he had ever made towards mechanisation being the purchase of a truck and two motorbikes. All of which had been acquired to assist on the station when they were shorthanded or extra busy, not for pleasure.

She shivered as Scott strapped her in beside him, no mercy on his face for those weaker than himself. Not a word had been spoken between them since they left the house. It seemed to Sherry that even the heat of the afternoon was chilled by his silent anger.

'Where are we going?' she asked, after surviving what was, for her, the soul-shaking experience of taking off. Her voice was little more than a whisper, but he heard.

'Bourke,' he replied.

'What makes you think they've gone there?'

'Just a feeling I have,' he levelled out grimly. 'If they intend getting married, I believe they might be inclined to do it as soon as possible, knowing I wouldn't be far behind. Considering everything, Bourke seems the most likely place.'

'What about Broken Hill?'

'Ellen knows I went there this morning, and wouldn't risk it. The unlikely million-to-one chance sometimes happens.'

Sherry cast an apprehensive glance at him. She felt terrible. Her body felt cold and stiff and full of bitter protests she didn't dare utter. She found it difficult to comprehend Kim's elopement, but Scott refused to believe her shock was as great as his.

Despite the pain Kim was causing her, she still felt compelled to try and help the runaway couple. 'D-don't you think,' she stammered, 'if Kim and Ellen are determined to marry each other and things have gone this far, it would be better to let them?'

'No.'

So uncompromising. It was the jaw and chin, the hard mouth, reflecting an unforgiving nature. This man would bear grudges—and how! Sherry's eyes flashed as she turned away. Scott Brady was a magnificent-looking man. If only he would unbend a little. If she had been Kim and Ellen she would have been terrified! As it was, it was going to be bad enough being Sherry Grant, before this was over.

She said carefully, 'As they're both over age, could you actually do anything to stop them?'

'If I reach them in time,' he bit out, 'I can do a lot.'

'Well, if you could,' she snapped, suddenly angry, 'Why didn't you do something sooner?'

'I thought I'd done everything necessary,' he retorted coldly. 'I put the fear of death into Ellen and thought I had her under constant observation.'

'You imagined you had!'

'I rarely leave anything to chance, Miss Grant.

Someone's head is going to roll! However, I did try, whereas you didn't.'

'What was I supposed to do, for heaven's sake?' she cried hoarsely. 'I pointed out the disadvantages of marriage between them, every chance I got. Whatever you might think, I did my best.'

He glanced at her, his face cruel, without a trace of compassion in the savage twist of his lips. 'It's a bit late to try and impress me with your innocence, Sherry. I suggest you sit back and shut up while I land.'

Even as a complete novice to small plane flying she recognised expertise when she saw it. Scott brought the plane down so smoothly, she scarcely felt a bump, exhibiting the same skill he applied at almost everything. Taxiing off the runway, he told her, with a grimness she hadn't the courage to defy, to stay where she was.

Watching his tall figure striding away from her, Sherry began sobbing with reaction. How could Kim have done this to her? If Scott did but know, she was too frightened to move an inch. Frantically she stemmed her tears. She didn't want to think what Scott might do if he caught Kim and Ellen, but weeping wouldn't help. She supposed, reasonably, he couldn't commit murder, but he might easily dish out its near equivalent.

As the minutes dragged slowly by, Sherry's mind was besieged by future problems as well as immediate ones. If Scott washed his hands of the unfortunate couple, which he would do, undoubtedly, she just couldn't see Ellen settling happily at Googon. It wasn't just a case of adjusting, one had to be fair. Grandfather had never done a thing to improve the house. It was adequate but basic. He had always held the view that a small grazier could live happily for a lifetime by under-stocking and spending as little as possible of what he made. Certainly such a theory was upheld in times of drought when he had both grass and money saved to buy extra fodder, but that might be no consolation to Ellen if she had to slave over an old-fashioned stove!

Sherry wondered how she had adapted so surprisingly well, from sheer luxury to an almost complete lack of comfort. Was it because she had been so young? That Kim hadn't shared her ability to make the best of it had long been apparent, so how could he expect Ellen to? Even as she trembled for him, Sherry couldn't remember feeling so despairing of her brother.

When Scott returned she didn't like the look on his face at all. Numbly she gazed at him, too apprehensive to speak, a frozen question in her eyes.

He didn't attempt to spare her. 'I have reason to believe they were married here, this afternoon, and left for Brisbane a few hours ago.'

Sherry stared at him blankly. 'So Kim's now your brother-in-law?'

She didn't know what made her say such a thing, she could have bitten her tongue out. It was one of those idiotic remarks, torn from a mind too shocked to come up with anything sensible. A false reaction, like laughing when one really feels like crying.

Scott wasn't making allowances. He looked as if he'd have liked to have slapped her again. 'You'd better not congratulate yourself too soon, Sherry. I haven't finished with them yet.'

Her eyes widened as she bit her lip. 'I shouldn't have said that.'

'You shouldn't,' he snapped, 'but triumph isn't easy to restrain.'

He would just have to believe it. Incredulously she asked, 'Are you sure they're married?'

'Almost as sure as I can be.' The grey eyes were glacial. 'We're going to find out.'

'We?' Her pale, pinched face looked askance at him.

As though brute force might explain it, Scott grasped her by her slender waist to haul her down beside him. While she was still searching for her depleted breath, he told her grimly, 'I've chartered a jet. It will get us to Brisbane as quick as anything.'

Again, the only thought to cross her mind had nothing to do with her present predicament. 'It's a wonder you don't have one of your own!'

It was necessary to keep on fighting him or weep, but she was startled when he retorted, 'I did have.'

'Had?'

He slanted her a glance, taunting with derision as he dragged her in the direction of the other plane, 'You sound as if you see a poor man beside you, Sherry, and your hopes of a prosperous future disappearing. I merely decided I could be killing myself by inches, continually chasing round the world, so I sold a few of my companies. What I have left eliminates the need for fast jets and enables me to stay at home.'

'You must still have one on stand-by?'

The pace he was going didn't slacken, although he must hear she was breathless. 'I have shares in an airline company which obliges me sometimes. This evening we've been lucky.'

That wasn't the word Sherry would have chosen! Disastrous might have been more appropriate! With Scott so close on their heels, Kim and Ellen mightn't stand a chance of evading him. He wasn't prepared to be forgiving or even tolerant, and though her own sympathy with the runaway couple was fast fading, she shuddered to think what might happen to them when Scott found them.

CHAPTER FIVE

THE small jet, piloted by expert staff, got them to Brisbane in no time. All the way Sherry felt sick, but even had she been at death's door she doubted if Scott would have taken any notice. He was silent with an icy fury she could almost feel, and while underneath it, he might be concerned for his sister as well, his consuming feelings were those of anger.

He would never allow that she was as disturbed as he was. Glancing at him frequently, Sherry was terrified by the grimness of his face. Though still reeling with shock she was trying to resign herself to making the best of things, but Scott's thoughts were clearly fixed on revenge.

She was so upset she took little notice of the country over which they were flying. The drier saltbush plains of the Darling Basin round Bourke gave way, as they crossed the border into Queensland, to the wheat paddocks and grazing lands of the Darling Lowlands, where some of Australia's finest cattle, sheep and racehorses are bred. They were soon over the Great Dividing Range, which stood sentinel over the entire length of Queensland and swooping down on the capital, eighty miles away.

Just before they landed at Brisbane Airport, Sherry tried once more to appeal to Scott. Distractedly she asked, 'Why are you so against this marriage?' Unwisely she probed further. 'Is it because your own failed?'

His eyes cursed her and she supposed she deserved his reply. 'My own marriage failed, Sherry, because my wife didn't like my sexual appetites.'

Sherry went scarlet and she guessed he had shocked

77

her deliberately. Being so blunt about matters he must know she had little experience of was one way of telling her he no longer considered her feelings. Her hot cheeks might have betrayed her, but she was determined to pretend she had as much sophistication as he had. Which might thwart him better than revealing her true state of mind.

As calmly as possible she retorted, 'You couldn't have been very gentle with her.'

'My God,' Scott laughed tautly, 'you can't know how gentle I was! I would never be so considerate again.'

'Maybe she wasn't ex-experienced . . .'

He broke in cynically, before she could sink further into a self-made morass, 'You could be right. Before she met me, she confessed she'd been to bed with only a few men and never yet found one who didn't disgust her.'

'Oh.' Defeated, Sherry lowered her thick lashes in confusion, yet she couldn't help wondering how any woman married to a man like Scott Brady wouldn't welcome his attentions. Incoherently she mumbled, 'That's why you divorced her?'

'Correction,' he snapped, 'she divorced me. Now she spends her time working for women's rights.'

'You shouldn't let it make you bitter,' she whispered.

'Bitter!' Again his glacial glance froze her. 'Being a gentleman, I allowed my name to be dragged through the mud of the divorce courts, but I count myself plain damned lucky to be rid of her.'

Feeling too bewildered to find a suitable comment, Sherry was relieved when they reached their destination. As they left the airport, to travel the four miles to the city, she asked nervously, 'Have you any idea where they might be?'

'If they're here,' Scott said curtly, 'there are a couple of possibilities. Otherwise it could take longer.'

Expecting he would be taking her with him, since he seemed unwilling to let her out of his sight, she was startled when he added, 'I'm taking you to a hotel before I begin looking.'

'Won't I be going with you?'

'No,' his voice was uncompromisingly firm, 'I want to see them alone first.'

'First?'

'Afterwards I'll bring them to see you.'

'W-will they want to see me?' she faltered, uncertain of her own feelings.

'The outcome will be interesting,' he said enigmatically, leaving her to wonder what fiendish thoughts were going through his head. What pleasure could he hope to derive from such a meeting? Did he intend making them all grovel?

He had evidently instructed their driver before leaving the airport, because the taxi stopped outside a huge hotel. It was so large, one might stay here without being noticed, and she guessed that was why Scott had chosen it. He asked for a room, not rooms, but she made no comment. It made her feel anxious, but her weariness was suddenly too great to allow her to worry on that account. And finding Kim and Ellen could take him all night.

He escorted her to the lift, after a porter who was obviously wondering why they had no luggage. As Sherry flushed uncomfortably at what he must be thinking, Scott's hand dug in the middle of her back. 'I won't run away!' she breathed.

He didn't answer or even glance at her, but she saw his mouth tighten. His fingers might be burning into her skin, but he didn't seem aware of it. They were conducted to one of the best rooms when the porter left them, after enquiring if there was anything else they required.

She expected Scott to leave as well, but he came in and closed the door. Her blue eyes searched his face in silent enquiry, and she felt a flutter of apprehension as he stood regarding her silently. He was able to make her heart beat faster just by looking at her, she was discovering, and was mortified to realise he knew it.

'What did you tell them at reception?' she asked, her mind in chaos again.

His brows rose. 'I merely asked for single accommodation. I'm in no mood to think up plausible explanations, which no one would believe anyway.'

'The receptionist recognised you.'

'So what? I've stayed here before.' The grey eyes were hard and brilliant, without mercy as he suddenly dragged her to him. His face was cruel as he totally disregarded her startled cry. Before his mouth came down on her parted lips, his glance slid over them, contemptuously brooding.

As Sherry struggled to free herself of the drugging onslaught of that kiss, sparks from the leaping fire of Scott's passion spread to her own body. She moaned helplessly, a curious weakness invading her, her bones melting as his hands began travelling sensuously over her. Her mind stopped functioning to the extent that she suffered severely from shock as he swiftly thrust her away.

She shook her head violently, as if to deny her own response, but gazed at him blankly as he spoke. 'Do you believe I would really touch you? That little demonstration was merely to set your narrow little mind at rest. I couldn't leave you as easily if I had any intention of seducing you. You're flattering yourself if you think I'd be foolish enough to risk any further involvement with your despicable family. Do you imagine I would put another weapon in your brother's hands?'

Her face paled. She could understand his reasoning but not his methods. 'Don't worry,' she replied fiercely, 'I'm getting very tired of being used—by both you and Kim. In staying here, with you, I was only thinking of my reputation.'

'Have you one to lose?'

She knew he was implying other things as well, but she was too tired to fight him. If he appeared to have forgotten, at least briefly, what he had come to Brisbane for, she hadn't.

Ignoring his derisive query, she said stiffly, 'What about Kim and Ellen? Aren't you interested in finding them any more?'

'Naturally,' he rejoined curtly, his eyes on her white face, 'but before I go I want your promise you'll be here when I return.'

So that was why he had waited, She laughed mirthlessly. 'You have my promise, for what it's worth.'

She meant, for what he considered it worth, and he nodded harshly. 'I have no choice but to trust you. Don't think I give a damn where you run to, but any city can be dangerous at night.'

'I wouldn't know where to run to,' she replied tautly, 'and I didn't bring much money.'

'Just as well,' he said curtly. 'While I'm gone, I advise you to get some rest if you can't sleep.'

When the door closed behind him, Sherry sank down on the bed. Her nerves were strung so tight, for a moment she feared for her sanity. It took several deep breaths to ward off the feeling of panic. Despondently she glanced round the room, which after only minutes was beginning to feel like a prison. It was large and luxurious with a bathroom attached, the kind of hotel room many dream of but can seldom afford. The carpets and curtains were beautiful, while the covers on the bed were of the finest silk.

Eventually, when weariness completely overcame her, Sherry slipped off her shoes and stretched out on the bed, staring at the ceiling. She would have given a lot for a cup of tea, but while she supposed there was room service, she didn't ring for anything.

After a while she dozed, wakening to find two hours had passed. It was after midnight and she wondered

how long Scott would be. If he was bringing Ellen and
Kim back with him she would need to have her wits
about her. Feeling anything but bright, she decided to
take a shower in order to revive herself a little. It
shouldn't take more than a few minutes. She was just
drying herself when she heard a key turn in the outer
door and Scott strode in.

She recognised his step and gasped in alarm. 'Sherry?'
she heard him call impatiently.

'I won't be a minute!' she cried hastily.

Sensing he was alone, she felt a return of her former
panic. Why hadn't he brought Kim and Ellen? He
wouldn't have come back if he hadn't found them!
Blindly, Sherry simply threw a towel round herself and
stumbled into the bedroom.

At a glance she saw her fears were well founded.
Scott was indeed alone. In vain her eyes searched and
putting the back of a hand against her mouth, she bit
hard to regain control. 'Where are they?' she asked
unsteadily. 'Didn't you find them?'

'Yes.' His voice was clipped as his glance swept over
her. 'You can dress first, if you like.'

'No!' Her voice rising, she was beside him, clutching
his arm, unaware of the abandoned picture she made,
the towel covering little of her slender body, her dark
hair streaming over her shoulders.

As she swayed and her startling blue eyes threatened
to engulf her face, Scott drew a harsh breath while his
mouth thinned. 'I found Ellen,' he said, as she silently
entreated him to go on. 'We have an apartment here
that she sometimes uses. I almost didn't go as I thought
it would be too obvious.'

Sherry was shaking so much she could hardly get
another question past her lips. 'They are married?'

Scott laughed, with such acridity, she shrank from
him. He replied flatly, his eyes icy with anger, 'Ellen is
married, all right, but not to your brother.'

Sherry must have fainted. When she came round she

was lying on the bed with Scott bending over her, trying
to revive her.

'I'm all right,' she moaned, everything coming back
in a flash. 'What did you say about Kim?'

'Later,' he said tersely.

She hadn't noticed he was gently massaging her nape.
The towel had slipped from her shoulders halfway to
her waist. 'Oh!' she cried, crimsoning as she felt his eyes
on her small but perfect breasts. Her body began to
tremble and for the second time that night she was
utterly bewildered by the feelings he aroused in her.
'Please don't touch me,' she whispered, quite incapable
of stopping him herself.

His head lifted and his mood frightened her as she
felt the desire to hurt which raged in him. 'You're right
to be worried,' he grated savagely. 'When I thought you
might be my brother-in-law's sister, that put you out of
bounds. Now you're the sister of my sister's despicable
accomplice, I intend taking you some time, if only for
revenge.'

'Scott!' Half sobbing, her face white, she trembled as
the hard pressure of his hands forced her back against
the pillows. She knew he was considering taking her
there and then, as some terrible violence increased
inside him, demanding release. He wanted to invade her
body, to crush her to a vortex of mindless response and
feverish flesh. Every movement he made was so full of
dark intent that she felt terrified. 'Scott,' she repeated,
as his threats made her almost faint again, 'what do you
mean? How can Ellen be married, if not to Kim?'

He was angry, burning with rage because, perhaps
for the first time in his life, someone had made a fool of
him. 'She married Barry White's foreman, one Rory
Kingsley Grant, commonly known as Red, owing to the
colour of his hair.'

Sherry couldn't recall a day when she'd had so many
shocks altogether. She stared at Scott in horror, quite
forgetting she was lying half naked under his

unrelenting hands. 'I don't understand!' she breathed hoarsely. 'I thought Ellen was in love with Kim. Didn't she tell you she was going to marry him?'

'Yes,' he nodded grimly, 'and I believed her, which was what I was supposed to do.'

The self-mockery in his voice was all too evident and Sherry felt even more confused. 'But what about Kim?' she cried. 'Or was she deceiving him, too?'

'No,' his face tightened. 'I wouldn't have felt so bad about him if she had been. Apparently he was helping her to mislead me.'

Sherry couldn't believe it. 'Was it his idea?'

He stared into her anguished, incredulous eyes. 'It appears she got upset one evening when she was telling him about Red. She knew I would never approve and it was something impulsive they dreamed up together.'

Completely stunned, Sherry shook her head. 'I can imagine Kim enjoying the possibilities of such a scheme, but I find it difficult to believe he would take it seriously.'

'Doesn't the evidence speak for itself?'

Sherry nodded numbly. She couldn't dispute it, but while she was aware of Kim's faults, she wouldn't have thought deceiving people was one of them. 'Have you any idea why?' she asked helplessly.

'Seemingly, according to Ellen, he didn't like the way I patronised him.'

'You—you did a bit,' Sherry said hesitantly.

'Sherry,' said Scott, in flat controlled tones, 'we could spend hours looking for reasons. He was probably bored and fed up, wanting acclamation before he earned it, but none of that can possibly justify what he did. I consider his part in this affair an outrageous invasion of my family privacy.'

Distraught, Sherry gazed up at him, and he stared back at her. Something quivered between them and his eyes darkened formidably as he rejected whatever it was. Sherry knew she wasn't thinking constructively—

but how could she, with a mind torn by shock jumping distractedly from one thing to another?

'Aren't you taking any responsibility?' she asked jerkily. 'You didn't approve of Kim, but surely the man Ellen's married must have something to recommend him if he was Barry White's overseer? You must have given her some cause to believe you wouldn't accept him either?'

For a moment Sherry thought he wasn't going to answer, but he did. 'Months ago I found her flirting with him at a barbecue the Whites were giving. I thought she was merely amusing herself.'

'You didn't say anything?'

'I said plenty,' Scott admitted, without noticeable signs of regret. 'I said enough to leave her in no doubt as to what I thought of her behaviour.'

'With someone you considered unsuitable?'

The sarcasm in her voice didn't escape him, but he merely nodded. 'I've told you before, Sherry, Ellen's probably a victim of her environment, she's both idle and extravagant, and I can't see her reforming overnight. Grant can never hope to support her, as I've done for years, and I don't look forward to keeping the two of them.'

'Maybe her husband doesn't want to be kept,' Sherry pointed out. 'And doesn't Ellen have anything of her own?'

'Nothing to speak of,' he replied curtly. 'My father left very little.'

Which must prove that the rumours of Scott's Midas touch weren't completely without foundation! Yet surely he wouldn't see his own sister starving? And if he hadn't been so busy making money he might have seen what was going on!

Wearily Sherry brushed some hair from her face, surprised to find her skin deathly cold. Again her thoughts jumped erratically.

'Didn't you realise in Bourke that it wasn't Kim she'd married?'

'No,' he retorted grimly. 'I was told she had married someone called Kingsley Grant, who I naturally assumed was your brother. Ellen had obviously seized on the coincidence of similar names and traded on it. Unfortunately I didn't wait to make further enquiries.'

'And—in all this, Kim aided and abetted her?'

'One way of putting it,' he agreed contemptuously.

The madness of it all made Sherry feel more like collapsing every minute. It was becoming rapidly more difficult to think straight. Suddenly it occurred to her that she had no idea where Kim was. If he hadn't married Ellen, why hadn't he returned to Googon?

'Do you know where Kim is?' she asked unsteadily.

Scott's eyes flashed as though he wished he did, while the sudden clenching of his hands suggested he wouldn't have minded them round Kim's neck. 'According to Ellen, after the ceremony he left for Sydney.'

'Sydney?'

He hesitated, but only a second, before twisting the knife. 'Then London.'

'Oh, no!'

His eyes reflected a cruel satisfaction as Sherry's face went whiter. 'I imagined he might want to put some distance between us, but not that much.'

Sherry couldn't take it in. She hugged the towel round her quivering body, immune to the derisive glitter in Scott's eyes as she drew it over her breasts. 'Wh-what about Googon?' she cried.

'You'll have to ask your brother that,' Scott said indifferently, 'when he gets in touch.'

In the meantime, what am·I to do? Sherry wondered feverishly. Fright welled up inside her, feelings of absolute terror. Everything was hitting her like an avalanche. She felt abandoned, betrayed, utterly desolate. Kim had lied to her for weeks, letting her believe he was in love with Ellen, all the wrong things. He had been amusing himself at everyone's expense!

'He can't have realised what he was doing!' she cried hoarsely, thinking he couldn't possibly, otherwise he couldn't have carried on.

'Don't try and make excuses for him,' Scott rasped furiously. 'If you're going to worry, I suggest you begin worrying over yourself, because someone's going to pay for his sins. I might have overlooked a lot if your brother had been emotionally involved, but to deliberately assist a girl to deceive her own family is beyond comprehension.'

Sherry stared at him like a frightened child, her lips quivering as she saw the blazing rage on his face. She guessed this whole thing had been distasteful to him from the beginning. Other men might enjoy such dramatics as Ellen indulged in, but Scott Brady believed in discretion. His affairs with women might be hot-blooded, but the world at large would never know of them. Helplessly Sherry bit her lip, wondering what he meant by threatening that she might have to pay for Kim's sins. Surely he knew she had no money? Remembering his earlier threats, she shivered, but refused to take them seriously.

'What will Kim do in England?' she muttered, talking to herself.

Scott said mockingly, 'Aren't you wondering if he's not asking himself what will you do here?'

Sherry found a flicker of defiance. 'I'll stay at Googan, of course, until he comes back.'

'If he ever does.'

Faintly, Sherry allowed, 'You have a right to feel bitter.'

'Your brother helped ruin my sister's life.'

Kim had acted badly, so badly that Sherry realised it might be a relief not to see him again for a while, but she couldn't believe Ellen's life was ruined. She suspected Ellen wasn't nearly as helpless as Scott imagined her to be.

Drawing a steadying breath, she said, 'Kim shouldn't

have done what he did, Scott, but I can't agree that Ellen's marriage won't work out. What would you do if you fell in love with someone you considered your social inferior?'

He glanced at her mockingly. 'I would certainly not deprive myself,' his eyes flicked over her so she flushed as she understood his meaning, 'but I certainly wouldn't marry her. As for Ellen's marriage, we'll just have to wait and see, won't we?'

'I—I just hope you won't be too hard on her,' Sherry murmured, not sure why she was pleading leniency for a girl who had shown her so little consideration.

Scott shrugged, appearing to lose interest in his sister. 'I told you, you'd be wiser to worry about yourself. Have you had any dinner?'

His abruptness was confusing. 'No,' Sherry remembered, 'I wasn't hungry.'

'I was, but I didn't have time to eat.' Lithely he rose to his feet. 'I'll ring for coffee and sandwiches. If they arrive while I'm having a shower, let them in.'

Her breath shortened. 'You mean here?'

'Why not?' He began removing his jacket and tie. 'You can get anything if you're willing to pay for it.' As his jacket landed on the bed he lifted the house phone and rapped an order. 'There,' he said, as though she was a child, 'it's very easy, really.'

'That's not what I meant!' Sherry huddled deeper in her towel, feeling trapped by it. 'I meant what will they think? We aren't husband and wife.'

'Nor ever will be.'

Was he being deliberately obtuse? 'My reputation!'

'So you're still on about that?'

Hating his sarcasm, she hissed, 'Contrary to what you seem to believe, I do have one!'

Scott sighed, his manner long-suffering. 'We can agree to differ over it, surely? All I want is some coffee, and you look as if you could do with some yourself, by the looks of you! Today, thousands of unmarried couples stay in hotels and no one thinks anything of it. And hotel staff aren't paid to censure the guests.'

Realising the futility of arguing with him, she said stiffly, 'Very well, but I'll have to get dressed.'

'I'm doing my best to get undressed,' he said dryly. 'I'd like a shower before the coffee arrives. You'd better wait until I've finished, then you can have the bathroom. Unless you can manage in here?'

Sherry shook her head. She wasn't going to be caught scrambling guiltily into her clothes by some supercilious waiter! 'Please be quick!' she snapped, averting her eyes as Scott pulled off his shirt.

He closed the bathroom door with a derisive bang, but opened it again almost immediately. 'You'll have to give me your towel. It appears to be the only one.'

'It's all I've got!' she protested.

'It's all there is,' he insisted, whipping it without compunction from her shaking shoulders and returning the way he'd come.

'Oh, please, someone help me!' Sherry whispered feverishly, her eyes suddenly tear-drenched. Swiftly, as her prayers remained predictably unanswered, she dived under the sheets. Everything was getting out of hand. She was talking to herself, she couldn't even think properly.

Apprehensively, she stayed where she was, until there was a knock on the door. Aware that it must be someone with the refreshments, she was about to tell them to come in, when Scott returned and saved her the bother. She stared aghast, as he sat down again on the bed with only a towel draped round his waist, as the waiter entered at his command, leaving them a tray.

Before he left, she saw the man's glance flicker over the clothes scattered on the bed and could almost have died with shame.

'I'll tell you something!' she lashed out at Scott, when he had gone, her small face blazing. 'After tonight I

don't want to see any of you again. Not you, not Ellen,
or Kim! I hate the lot of you . . .!'

As her voice rose shrilly, Scott grasped her. 'You
little fool!' he exclaimed. 'Calm down. Are you trying to
raise the whole hotel?'

She couldn't calm down. Everything was becoming
too much for her. She began sobbing wildly, losing
control. 'I hate you—hate you!' she cried, repeating it
over and over again.

'No, you don't,' he snapped back, trying to hold her
still, with arms that threatened to break her in two.

Despite this, she kept on trying to hit him, not caring
what she was doing.

Suddenly, as if his patience was exhausted, Scott
whipped aside the sheets covering her. Taking no notice
of her enraged gasp, as her bare body collided with his,
he drew her ruthlessly to him. He looked down at the
way they were clamped together, his face totally devoid
of expression, and when he spoke his voice was
completely without kindness.

'The best cure for something is often a dose of the
same thing. You received a shock, today, so shall we
experiment?'

With a smile of pure mockery, he bent to her lips,
taking them with a certainty that proclaimed, without
doubt, that he was a man who knew what he was doing.

'No!' Sherry gasped, but it was too late. There was no
escape. His fingers tangled in the silky skeins of her
dark hair, tugging her head back, allowing him more
freedom to plunder. A surging warmth sent her blood
racing as his tongue traced the delicate contours of her
lips, alternately teasing and probing until she was weak
with longing. By the time his kiss deepened her
trembling mouth was opening to the increasing demand
of his and a blaze of something alien swept through her,
amazingly demolishing the aftermath of the afternoon.
Fright and desolation would surely return, but the
emotions flowing through her now were of a different

kind. Being purely physical they provided the temporary distraction she needed, to give her time to return to a more normal keel.

Sherry's senses reeled as Scott's arms tightened and she clung to him, unable to suppress a small moan. She became conscious of nothing but his heart thudding into hers and the hard, hot pressure of his mouth. A flame of desire ignited her whole body as he cupped her breasts in his hands and his tongue touched the aroused peaks. When his mouth returned to hers with mounting passion and he pulled her further under him, she began dissolving in fluid heat. Swiftly the first warmth of her response changed to a wild abandonment, which would have shocked her afresh, had she been capable of rational thought. Passionately she strained against him, delighting in the hurting hardness of his strong limbs and arms.

She didn't know how long it was before he stopped kissing her and eased away from her.

'Much as I might like to continue this pleasurable interlude,' he said firmly, 'it might be wiser to call a halt.'

It wasn't relief that dilated Sherry's pupils as she forced her eyes open in an effort to agree with him. She looked at him, her eyes wide and startled but with something in them, an innocence now tinged with curiosity, an awakening desire for something she had, as yet, no experience of. She couldn't understand how, still under the influence of the emotions Scott had aroused in her, she immediately felt calmer. The frightening feeling of tension had gone.

Unconsciously, mutely appealing, she raised her arms towards him again, but he drew back with a few curt words.

'Stop when you're winning, Sherry. You're feeling better, because we hadn't quite reached the point of no return.' When she began to protest, he didn't allow it. 'Come on,' he said ruthlessly, 'coffee!'

Re-tying the knot in the towel round his waist, he poured it out. Sherry, clutching the sheet about her once more, gazed with a bewildered resentment at his broad chest, trying not to remember how its roughness had felt against her. He implied that she had been winning. Who could ever hope to win against a man like him? she thought blankly.

After adding both sugar and cream to Sherry's coffee, he handed it to her with a sandwich. She noticed he left his own coffee black and drank a cupful straight off before he began on the sandwiches. His appetite, she remembered his taunts, was apparently not all sensual, though instinct told her that despite the tight control he kept over himself, he had enough libido for two men.

For all the temporary truce between them, she wasn't able to eat much and there was plenty left.

'Do you think you can sleep now?' asked Scott, putting the tray aside.

'Sleep? Where?' She began trembling again.

Scott looked at her and frowned. 'Stop it, Sherry. If I'd wanted to seduce you, I've had the chance. We have a bed big enough for half a dozen and it's only two in the morning. I don't intend passing the next few hours in a chair.'

'I could.'

'We'll both sleep here!' he said curtly.

How could he expect her to? Yet she hadn't the strength to fight him any more, not now anyway. The old tremors were returning, the panicky feelings.

'If you promise——' she began haltingly.

'Miss Grant,' he cut in dryly, 'I can't recall having slept in the past forty-eight hours. Last night I had a business crisis which kept me on the telephone until I decided it wasn't worth going to bed, and believe me, I'm human enough to feel the strain of what's happened tonight. I don't think I'd be capable of making love to anyone.'

Reassured, Sherry settled on the other side of the

bed, as far from Scott as possible. She would wait until he was asleep, then get quietly up and dressed, but the next thing she remembered it was dawn and to her horror she was curled up against him. Moreover, one of his arms was curved round her waist and the rough edge of his unshaven, aggressive chin grazed her forehead as her head lay on his shoulder.

Moving with great care, she edged from under his encirling arm, resisting all temptation to stay where she was. Her whole body flooded with embarrassment as she thought of how they must have slept in each other's arms. When she had dozed off there had been a respectable distance between them. She might have known that in sleep her body would naturally gravitate towards Scott's, but she had never slept with a man before.

Slipping out of bed, she scooped up her clothes and dived into the bathroom. After locking the door, she showered quickly, wishing the cold needles of water could wash away all contact of Scott's body. She had no make-up with her and after dressing could only sweep her hair back in a thick plait, but at least she felt clean.

On returning to the apartment, she was startled to find Scott about to leave it. She must have disturbed him when she got up, for, like herself, he was dressed, and she had only been gone a few minutes.

He halted when she appeared, his hand on the door. His eyes searched her pale face intently. 'How are you feeling?'

'All right.' She matched the coolness of her voice with a careless shrug, happier when his eyes hardened.

'I'm off in search of a shave,' he said abruptly. 'Shouldn't be long.'

He wasn't. She had scarcely regained her composure when he returned, his chin smooth again. Sherry wrenched her wistful glance from it to the dampness of his hair which indicated he had showered as well.

'We'll have breakfast,' he stated decisively, 'then make for the airport. I promised Andrew, that's our pilot, I'd be there early.'

'What if we hadn't found Ellen?' she exclaimed.

Scott's mouth thinned, making Sherry regret her impulsive query. 'I'd have let Andrew know.'

During breakfast he spoke very little and she found it difficult to associate the aloof, arrogant man sitting opposite her at a table in the hotel restaurant with the one who had held her in his arms all night. Obviously that episode was to be discounted. She need only remember his anger over Kim, that he disliked and disapproved of her because she was Kim's sister. The icy coldness of his eyes keeping her at a distance made her believe she could count herself lucky that he had gone no further than a few kisses, for even these had merely been an expression of his contempt.

CHAPTER SIX

'WILL you be busy when you get home?' Sherry asked stiffly, as later they flew out of Brisbane. Scott might consider it a ridiculous question, but she couldn't stand the silence between them any longer. As a rule she didn't mind silence, but this one was getting on her nerves.

'I'm giving a dinner party this evening,' he replied curtly. 'Ellen arranged it and it's too late to cancel.'

Wondering why he had told her, Sherry said uncertainly, 'You—you'll miss having her as your hostess.'

'For God's sake, girl, don't stammer over it,' he snapped. 'We both know that won't be her responsibility any more. I'll have to find someone else.'

'You mean—a wife?'

'I've been thinking about it anyway,' he said coolly. 'A man in my position needs a wife to help him entertain, and I believe I've enough experience now to choose someone eminently suitable.'

'Such as Miss Easten?'

He merely smiled with a hint of unmistakable satisfaction and asked her if she wouldn't like something to drink.

As he settled back again to silence, which this time she dared not break, Sherry had to allow the thoughts she had been keeping at bay since she woke up to intrude. All her anxieties flooded back, and somehow, strangely entangled with them, was the knowledge that there might soon be another mistress at Coomarlee.

So what? she asked herself impatiently. Being married again might humanise Scott Brady a bit, turn him into a more approachable neighbour. And, heaven help her, if

Kim didn't return she might need one! As for his kisses, the sooner she forgot them the better. Each time he had kissed her there had been a reason, but never the right one. He had never pretended to care for her and must dislike her now more than ever, for even her name would remind him of the man his sister had married.

The flight back to Bourke passed smoothly and once there they soon transferred to Scott's plane. In not many minutes they were landing at Googon again.

Scott helped Sherry to the ground but refused her offer of coffee. 'I'll have it at home,' he said, as he set her down, 'if you don't mind.'

Dully she shook her head. He was being polite, but he would never forgive her. She was suddenly thankful they weren't related, even by marriage.

She caught a flash of something she couldn't make out in his eyes and he seemed oddly reluctant to leave. As she turned away he caught her arm.

'I can't believe your brother would let a fear of repercussions drive him as far as the U.K. It might take a few days to revive his courage, but when he does return you might mention that I'd appreciate a word with him.'

'Of course.'

Scott's eyes narrowed on her white face. 'You sound sure he will return?'

She wasn't. She wasn't sure at all, but she had to pretend. Later she might be strong enough to face facts. 'I can't believe Kim is a coward, Mr Brady.'

'Scott will do,' his mouth twisted. 'It's a bit late for anything else. Do I take it your brother's never run away before?'

Sherry flushed with mortification, which she saw merely heightened his suspicions. 'I told you, Kim's no coward. When I tried to explain about my family you refused to listen, so now you must believe what you like.'

His eyes darkened with anger at her tone and he let

go of her arm. 'Goodbye, Miss Grant! But don't think it's for ever. If I don't see your brother, I'll certainly be seeing you!'

Trying to disregard Scott's frightening threats, Sherry trailed the few hundred yards to the homestead. She might have slept through the night, but she still felt very tired. There was no one about. Sam and the men would have been gone hours.

She went straight to the kitchen on entering the house, to make herself some coffee. To her surprise, on the long, scrubbed table lay a letter from Kim.

Only being able to hazard a guess as to how he had got it delivered so soon, she gazed at it in astonishment as she picked it up. If she hadn't recognised his handwriting she would never have believed it. Forgetting about coffee, she tore the letter open. It was from Kim. Where was he? she wondered frantically—why hadn't he come back himself?

'My dear Sherry,' he wrote, 'By the time you read this you may already have discovered I haven't married Ellen and am on my way to London. This will come as a shock and I'm sorry, but there's no way I can spare you.

'First, let me say I regret my involvement with Ellen. It was just one of those crazy things that happen without being planned. When it first came up I thought it would ease the boredom of a monotonous existence, as well as providing a chance to get back at Scott Brady. He's always regarded me as something inferior and since the crash at home I've felt very bitter and frustrated. These last weeks, though, I've come to rue agreeing to help Ellen deceive her brother, especially when I began realising how serious she was over this other chap. I couldn't let her down at the last minute, however, I had to see it through. I was best man at her wedding, but got no pleasure from it.

'As for London—well, Harold Gibson has, unknown to you, always kept in touch. At last he's managed to clear Dad's name. It wasn't his fault the crash happened, unless he was partly to blame for leaving his affairs too often in unscrupulous hands. There still won't be any cash, but that doesn't seem so important as that our debts have been settled. The crux of the matter is that Harold's been begging me to return. He isn't married and I think he has always looked on me as the son he never had. He has formed his own company, which he wishes to develop, and has invited me to join him, no capital required. (capital was heavily underlined) He's sure I can make it in a couple of years and I can't wait to try. The Outback isn't for me, Sherry, as you've probably guessed. I had to be sure, though—to make the decision myself. This was why I never said anything, and in the end there wasn't time to, but a quick, clean break might be best.

'Another thing, Sherry. I'd like you to remain at Googon, because it won't be convenient to have you with me in London. You should be able to survive for at least a year, which will give me a chance to concentrate on improving my position. You're far better with stock than I am and Sam will give you every assistance. And, by the way, I've spoken to Dan Cleary, the solicitor who, as you know, looked after Grandfather's affairs. He has promised to arrange about banking and things for you.'

There was more on this and further, rather complicated explanations regarding Ellen which got so involved as to make Sherry wonder if, despite everything, Kim hadn't been secretly hoping Ellen might eventually turn to him. He finished abruptly with a footnote.

'I had to sell the truck to help with travelling expenses and paying someone to deliver this. I hope you can manage until you find a replacement.'

Sherry was relieved that the men were out and there was no one to witness her distress. She couldn't cry, she felt beyond tears, but she had to slump down at the table for a while and bury her face in her hands, and she knew she must look ghastly. The shocks of the previous day and night had been great, but this was worse. Kim had done a lot of things, all inexcusable, and she was ready to sink through the floor with despair and shame.

He might have joined Ellen in a practical joke, but she couldn't forgive his skill as an actor, nor the lengths he had gone to to deceive people. She recalled the evening he had taken her out for dinner in Bourke. He had given the impression of being so hopelessly in love with Ellen that she had almost wept for him. And how many times had he let her painfully point out the disadvantages of bringing Ellen to Googon as a bride. He should do well in business, she thought bitterly, being so clever at hoodwinking people!

Kim didn't want her in London which, in all fairness, might be understandable, but Sherry couldn't help feeling rejected and alone. She might be able to manage Googon on her own, but how was she to face Scott Brady? Oddly enough, facing him seemed the much more formidable task. He must be within his rights in expecting some kind of apology from Kim. Now it appeared he wasn't going to get one and would be justified in branding Kim a coward along with other things! She wasn't sure why Scott's good opinion and forgiveness was suddenly important, but she sensed she might be miserable without it.

She had to be glad her father's name was cleared— but then she had always believed him innocent of the charges levelled against him. If anyone could lick Kim into shape it would be Harold Gibson, but she wouldn't like his task. Kim might have a good brain, but she was doubtful that he had the willpower to apply it. For Harold's sake, Sherry hoped he had!

Aware, owing to her present state of mind, that she must give herself time before making any important decisions, Sherry was, nevertheless, forced to make one or two. As her thoughts turned to Scott again, she remembered he wanted Googon. It struck her that, with Kim gone for good, there might be influences Scott could bring to bear to make her part with the property. She didn't doubt his power, if he chose to exercise it, and she might soon find herself homeless. It wasn't inconceivable that he might be able to force her to sell and it seemed imperative that she saw Dan Cleary before Scott heard about Kim. Until her own position was clarified it might be important that she didn't confide in anyone, not even Sam.

Hiding Kim's letter, she had another shower, hoping it would make her feel better before she made herself a cup of coffee and went back to Bourke. She must try and see Dan Cleary immediately. She didn't ring for an appointment. Knowing how evasive he had often been with Kim, she decided to take him by surprise.

The kettle had just boiled when the phone rang. To her dismay it was Scott. 'You all right?' he asked abruptly, after snapping his name.

'I—I'm fine!' she lied. 'You don't have to keep pretending you're concerned.'

'I'm only concerned for my own interests,' he retorted. 'As you're none the worse, apparently, for what you've been through, I want you for dinner tonight.'

'I assure you, Mr Brady, you'd have the most terrible indigestion.'

'Sherry!' his voice came sharper, 'don't play games— I've had enough of those from your brother. As Ellen's not here, I'm one short at the table, so you'll have to oblige.'

Her heart pounded unpredictably rapidly at the thought of seeing him again so soon. She replied unsteadily, 'I'm sure you must have plenty of friends willing to do that.'

'It's you I want, Sherry,' he was adamant. 'You owe it to me.'

'I—do?'

'Work it out for yourself.' He sounded as if he was running out of patience. 'I'll pick you up at seven.'

He gave her no time to explain about the truck. His high-handedness was infuriating! Yet, as she stared angrily at the dead receiver in her hands, Sherry was aware that two minutes' talk with Scott had done more to stiffen her backbone than any amount of showering had done. So this was one of the ways he intended punishing her for being a Grant? He was going to enjoy watching her sitting at his dinner table, seeing his other guests casting her curious, disparaging glances. Scott himself wouldn't spare her much thought. He would take pleasure from her discomfort in small doses, whenever he felt bored.

If she hadn't been extra sensitive over unpaid debts, Sherry would have refused to even think of going to Coomarlee. But as Kim wasn't going to be there to make any kind of recompense, she felt somehow bound to do what she could. As soon as she learned Kim's address in England, she would write and ask him to send Scott a letter of apology.

The only transport she could find to take her to Bourke was Sam's ancient runabout. Hoping he wouldn't mind her borrowing it, she set out. It proved a rough ride, with dust almost choking her, and to crown it all, nearly crashing into Dulcie Easten coming out of Scott's intersection. Knowing she was at fault didn't prevent Dulcie adopting the demeanour of the injured party. As Sherry swerved off the road to avoid her, Dulcie glared at her, shaking a fist in fury. In view of such outrage and the certain knowledge that Dulcie would never admit to being in the wrong, Sherry kept on going. If Dulcie had shown any sign at all of being reasonable, she would have tossed her for who should go first. If Dulcie had to eat the dust Sam's car was stirring all the way to Bourke, it might teach her to control her temper in future!

Feeling she had scored over Miss Easten didn't help Sherry's confidence, though, after she had parked and found Dan Cleary's office. Kim had suggested she could run Googon without much trouble for a year, and she had been half inclined to agree with him until she realised Dan Cleary might easily laugh that she was even thinking of it. He would discount all the experience she had picked up and relegate her to the ranks of a helpless, fanciful female. Like many Australian men, he liked to believe the little woman was all right in her place, but little use out of it.

Unfortunately, because she had come a long way, Dan wasn't available. He was in Sydney and his secretary invited her to make an appointment for the following day. Sherry hid her dismay and pretended to be grateful. It was her own fault. If she hadn't thought she was being clever, trying to take Dan unawares, she might have saved herself a hot and tedious journey.

On her way back to the car, she suddenly paused before a shop window. She wasn't paying attention to the stores, having been weighing up the advantages of seeing the bank manager before seeing Dan, then deciding against it. The blue chiffon dress in the shop window must have made an immediate impact, because it scattered her sober thoughts and stopped her in her tracks. It was beautiful, she smiled dreamily, imagining herself wearing it. The chiffon was so light and soft, it would suit her small, slender figure while the colour would almost exactly match her eyes. Her eyes widened wistfully and she sighed.

'Are you going to buy it?'

Startled, Sherry swung round, thinking it couldn't be happening that she was running into Miss Easten twice on the same day! It was Dulcie, however, looking quite pleased with herself this time.

'I'm sorry I gave you a fright back there,' Sherry mumbled.

The other girl accepted the apology Sherry had never

intended making as if it was her due. 'You should certainly drive more carefully. In fact,' she wondered shrewdly, 'I'm not sure that whatever it was you were driving is fit to be on the roads at all!'

Hastily Sherry turned again to the shop window. The point Dulcie was making was not one she felt able to argue with, and she didn't want to get Sam into trouble.

Dulcie's attention strayed to the dress too. 'That looks very nice,' she shrugged, 'but it's hardly the kind of thing you'd wear at Googon.'

Sherry swallowed the insult because she couldn't dispute the truth of it, yet a surge of resentment made her retort impulsively, 'I'm going out, this evening, and I do need a new dress. Do you think it would suit me?'

Incredibly she was talking to fresh air. Dulcie had disappeared, apparently inside the shop, as the door closed sharply. What a strange creature! Sherry gazed in bewilderment at the empty space where Dulcie had been. Dulcie's moods, like her appearances, were unpredictable. If Scott married her, would his second marriage be any happier than his first? Dulcie might make him an attractive wife, but Sherry doubted that she was as kind and warm-hearted as he believed her to be.

Still, Sherry wouldn't have considered Dulcie so irrational she would have taken off without at least one parting shot! With a last wistful glance at the beautiful creation in the shop window, Sherry continued along the street. She couldn't afford a new dress, anyway, it was stupid to pretend she could. And it wasn't any of her business whom Scott Brady married, nor did she care. It must be sheer imagination that even picturing him with another woman should make her heart ache.

She managed to get home and have dinner cooked for the men and dress before Scott called for her. She had to explain to Sam that though Kim hadn't married Ellen he might not be home for a while. This news, in itself, didn't appear to greatly bother him.

'The shearers will be coming next week, Miss Sherry,' Sam told her. 'We can manage, but he couldn't be away at a busier time.'

Sherry hesitated, conscious that Sam was waiting for her to say more. He knew there was more to say, but much as she would have liked to confide in him, she dared not confess Kim wasn't coming back until she had seen Dan Cleary.

Uncertainly she looked at him. 'I tried to see Dan Cleary today, Sam.' She had already apologised for borrowing his car but hadn't explained why. 'He's in Sydney, but I have an appointment tomorrow. After that we'll have to work something out, you and I . . .'

'Yes, Miss Sherry,' nodded Sam, looking at her so steadily, she understood he was trying to tell her she could count on him. 'I guess, until your brother returns, you want me to take over?'

As if Sam hadn't been running things since John Carey died! 'I'd be grateful. I'll give you all the help I can,' she added, looking so young and vulnerable that Sam frowned, then sighed.

Scott arrived five minutes early, surprising her by coming to fetch her himself when she had believed he might send one of his men. She had intended being at the door, whoever came, but he frustrated her by striding into the kitchen.

'Ready, Sherry?' he asked, as easily as if she had been going out with him regularly.

'Yes.' Because of Sam's presence, she forced a bright smile.

She still had to collect her handbag, and as she went to her room, the low murmur of Scott's voice followed her. Hoping he wasn't upsetting Sam with some derisive remarks on the poor condition of their stock, she hurried back.

The two men were talking, but their voices broke off when she reappeared. Sam said goodnight awkwardly, and Scott nodded and said he would keep in touch.

While this exchange was going on, Sherry glanced at Scott furtively. He was so tall and lean and powerful, he brought an immediate air of authority with him. Responsibility sat so easily on his broad shoulders that she could have cried with envy. He could run millions of acres without flinching, while even the thought of running a few thousand for a few months made her go weak at the knees.

Tearing her eyes from his ruggedly handsome features, she endured the hand he placed under her elbow to steer her out to the car.

'Heard from Kim yet?' he asked, after making sure she was comfortable.

'Can't we forget about him for one evening?' she hedged, rather than tell a lie.

Scott countered tightly, 'Until he returns, I assume you intend staying in the house alone?'

'Naturally,' she frowned. 'Sam and the boys are only a shout away.'

'Several hundred yards.'

'What were you saying to Sam, by the way?'

'Desperate to change the subject, aren't we?' he mocked. 'Did Sam look upset?'

'No, but I'm used to you poker-faced Australians! He might have been?'

'Ask him in the morning,' Scott taunted. 'I'm sure you'll find there's nothing wrong.'

Because he didn't mention Kim, or her sleeping alone again, she didn't persist. All kinds of awful premonitions were shaking her and she could almost feel the tension between them, but she sensed she might only make things worse if she annoyed him in any way. His mood seemed mild enough, but that could easily be a false front.

They covered the twelve miles to Coomarlee in as many minutes, and then Scott wasn't pushing the car any.

'I thought you would send one of your staff to collect me,' commented Sherry.

'I preferred to come myself.'

Some of his stock lay in the well irrigated paddocks round the homestead. Sherry tried not to look enviously at both the sheep and the land. Their arrival at Coomarlee coincided with that of the first of Scott's guests, and Sherry was aware of the curious glances which began as soon as she got out the car beside Scott.

'Now what is it?' he asked brusquely as she looked away with hot cheeks.

At his harsh tone, she caught her upper lip between her teeth. Fearing his anger, she shook her head but refused to look at him. 'I—I don't want to be the cause of undue speculation,' she stammered.

'Wait until you are before you worry,' he advised caustically.

Escorting her as far as the door, he left her with a murmur of excuse to go and meet Dulcie Easten. Sherry noticed how he helped Dulcie from her heavy vehicle with much more care than he had ever shown her. Despite the warmth of the evening, Dulcie was draped in a full-length fur cape that looked like mink. Whatever it was, Sherry was sure it had cost more than she might make off Googon in a whole year.

Unhappily she turned to follow with the other guests into the house as Scott and a graciously smiling Dulcie led the way. Scott appeared to have forgotten about Sherry Grant, and Sherry wished she could as easily forget him. If he hadn't been so attractive she might have done, but she was certain if she didn't see him again she might succeed in putting him from her mind. After this she must try and avoid him whenever possible, otherwise, she suspected hollowly, she might quickly fall a victim to his deceptive charm. He had kissed her, made light love to her, but she suddenly knew this was just the tip of the iceberg. He meant, in some way, to hurt her, and if she allowed herself to be lulled into a sense of false security by a few kisses, a

little warmth, how much easier it would be for him to
achieve his purpose. He would enjoy encouraging her,
but how much more pleasure would he get, after
perhaps rendering her like putty in his arms, from
rejecting her completely?

Because she hadn't brought a wrap, not having one
to bring, she was able to avoid Dulcie as she swept up
the impressive staircase at Coomarlee to dispose of her
things. People milled about her, shouting greetings to
old friends. Eventually they would sort themselves out
and someone would speak to her. Meanwhile, Sherry
felt uncomfortable, very de trop. As she stood to one
side, trying to look composed, Scott brought her a
drink.

'You look pale,' he frowned, yet his eyes were
insolent in their exploration, as they went over her. 'I
must say your clothes don't do much for you. You
looked better last night when you were sleeping.'

With practically nothing on? Did he have to remind
her—and without lowering his voice! 'Please!' her
cheeks burned with confusion and she couldn't look
around. 'Someone might hear you!'

'What of it?' he mocked. 'At least you've got a little
more colour.'

Sherry fretted in silence as he studied her face,
wishing she knew what he was looking for. He was
always so disapproving, she guessed he was trying to
pinpoint something else he could criticise. His face
was darkly brooding but full of the driving vitality
that alone could make her heart beat traitorously
faster. She stared into the odd intensity of his eyes as
a helpless weakness invaded her limbs, hating him for
daring to taunt her about something she would rather
forget. She had slept in his arms and responded when
he had kissed her, but she didn't want to be reminded
of it.

Despairingly she shook her head, attempting to get
rid of the feel of his arms, the taste of his mouth, still so

vivid he might have been kissing her now. The colour faded from her face and she went white again.

'What's wrong?' Scott's brows drew together.

Distraught, she could only stare at him, and her distress made him angry. With a glitter in his eyes, his hands descended on her shoulders. 'Tell me!'

She was so terrified of the emotions warring through her, she couldn't speak. Inside she was a mass of turbulence which seemed waiting remorselessly to get out of hand. Scott was staring at her trembling mouth, as though he would like to crush it to obedience beneath his own, and she knew if he did she would lose the last fraction of control.

They must be attracting attention. Scott wouldn't care, he never considered his actions in relation to what people might think, but Sherry didn't have his single-minded indifference. It struck her that he could be deliberately trying to divert attention from Ellen's absence, and she objected further to being used!

Her voice croaked but was audible. 'There's nothing wrong. I was simply thinking I'd rather have something long and cool to drink.'

Derision edging the thin curves of his mouth, Scott let go of her, at the same time removing the mercifully unspilt glass of sherry—which was all that was separating them. Sherry let him take it, relaxing the taut grip of her fingers on the delicate stem. In a matter of seconds, after Scott gave a clipped order to one of the maids, another glass was placed in her hands.

'I hope that's more to your liking?'

He sounded so sardonic that she suspected he had seen through her rather clumsy ploy to break up the tension between them. She nodded and looked away from him in bewilderment, shivering as a numb chillness took over her flesh. It wasn't possible she had fallen in love with him! Love shouldn't come like a bolt from the blue like this. Love should be a gentle flow of tender feelings. It shouldn't strike like a sword, so swiftly, without warning or mercy!

Sherry bent her head, like a frail flower on a long stem. How could one love a man one didn't understand? She had never had the chance to really know Scott Brady; it was only her senses that recognised him, as if they had known him for ever, even in another life.

Which must be extremely fanciful, to put it mildly! Much better to consider her feelings and Scott's indifference from a purely practical point of view. He was an enigma. Usually coolly aloof, he could be friendly enough when he chose, but it was only when he chose. He knew women and was able to give them much pleasure, but Sherry didn't think he had ever lost his head over a woman yet, not even his wife. He appeared to have no real regrets about his divorce, and if he had been wholly in love with her could he possibly be considering another marriage like a business proposition? Sherry knew she could never marry someone she didn't love, no matter how urgent her other needs were.

She heard Scott say curtly, 'Drink up.'

This had the apparently desired effect of raising her head and inviting further comment. 'You still have smudges under your eyes.'

As if he didn't know what had caused them! Rallying a little she glared at him. 'The past two days haven't been easy.'

'You're far too thin.'

'It's fashionable.'

Ignoring this, he continued studying her figure. 'You haven't lost all that in two days. I'd advise you to eat a good dinner.'

Tautly she retorted, 'I suppose it wouldn't do if I faded away before you had a chance to get your revenge?'

He didn't pretend not to understand. 'I said a lot of

things in anger, Sherry, which I believe, in the circumstances, was permissible.'

'You're still angry.'

'Up to a point.'

'May I interrupt?' a sugary voice begged sweetly. Taking permission for granted, Dulcie Easten slipped a possessive hand through Scott's arm. 'I'm sorry I took so long, darling, but my make-up was smudged and knowing how you like perfection, I had to repair it. I've just come down and someone said it looked as though you and Miss Grant were having an argument and they prevailed on me to intervene. They seemed to imagine Miss Grant was getting the worst of it!'

It irritated Sherry intensely that this was probably true, but she sensed that concern for Sherry Grant wasn't the real reason for Dulcie's intervention. She wasn't concerned, she was annoyed, and would be with any girl who appeared to be taking Scott's attention. Because of this, she said, deliberately provocative, 'Scott and I weren't arguing, Miss Easten. He was just making sure I was all right.'

Dulcie stabbed back in a way Sherry least expected. Glancing at Scott with an air of injured innocence, she exclaimed.

'Has this naughty child told you how she almost ran me off the road this morning, darling, just after I'd left here? She was driving some frightful vehicle, which I'm sure shouldn't have been on it. I mentioned it to Daddy and he's going to check. For her own good, of course,' she ended vaguely.

Scott frowned, clearly doing some quick thinking. 'What—vehicle?'

Sherry bit her lip. She would have liked to have avoided the question, but he was looking directly at her. 'I had to borrow Sam's runabout.'

'Who is Sam?' asked Dulcie quickly.

'Googon's foreman,' Scott replied absently, still

looking at Sherry. 'Why had you to borrow Sam's car, Sherry?'

As Sherry again hesitated, Dulcie put in quickly, without giving her a chance, 'I don't know why she had to borrow a car, darling, but I can guess why she went to Bourke. I found her there, admiring the very dress I'm wearing now, in a shop window. Because she was so rude to me, darling, I beat her to it, believing she deserved a lesson.'

In amazement, Sherry suddenly realised the dress Dulcie had on was indeed the same dress she had been admiring. She remembered thinking a few minutes ago, when Dulcie had first appeared, that there was something vaguely familiar about her, but she hadn't recognised what it was. She felt a sense of pique more than anger as she realised that if the dress fitted Dulcie it would have been far too big for her anyway. She might almost have been amused by the other girl's air of victory if she hadn't been so conscious of how shabby she must look by comparison.

Dulcie was pirouetting playfully while Scott looked on in grim-lipped silence. It wasn't until she asked him outright what he thought of her that he said dryly he thought she was very smart.

Clearly not wholly satisfied with his answer, Dulcie turned to Sherry again. 'It's a shame you didn't manage to find something else, although that old thing you're wearing looks very nice.'

Sherry, flushing painfully at Dulcie's veiled insult, was relieved when dinner was announced. Scott was obviously furious that she might have seriously injured his girl-friend. She shivered as he stared at her harshly. It would be yet another crime he would consider the Grants had committed against him.

Much to her surprise he placed her next to him at dinner, clearly disconcerting Dulcie and Mrs Fox, as well as herself. Had they but known it, Scott had a reason for having Sherry near him.

'What were you doing in Bourke today?' he asked conversationally.

Carefully she laid down her soup spoon, so it didn't clatter on her plate. The chilled gazpacho soup was delicious with its sprinkling of herbs, but had suddenly lost its taste. He was trying to catch her off guard, she realised. 'I couldn't settle at home . . .'

Contemptuously he disregarded her halting explanation. 'Can't you do better than that?'

'Please, Scott,' she lifted shadowed blue eyes to him, aware this was only his opening shot, 'not here!'

'As you wish.' He stared at her for another long moment before turning abruptly to speak to someone across the table.

The weak relief Sherry felt at such an easy victory persisted until after they had finished eating, when he asked her to step into the study with him.

'I'd rather not.' She went three shades paler, knowing he wouldn't accept a second excuse. He wanted to berate her over endangering Dulcie and she didn't know how much more she could take. If she could put him off a little longer, he might forget. Frantically she glanced past her shoulder towards a group of people she had been with. 'I promised I'd have coffee with some of your guests,' she babbled. 'I've just been talking to Simon and Mary Armstrong and they asked me to join them specially. They're going to Europe and spending a week in London, and they're interested that I used to live there.'

'Ah, yes,' he mused, eyes glinting silver, 'this trip they're taking at the end of the month. So they intend picking your brains, do they? You must just have been a child when you lived there. Do you think you'll be able to remember anything of interest to grown-ups?'

Sherry knew he was deliberately taunting her and hid her resentment behind a tilted chin. 'I'm sure I shall.'

'Run along, then.' He appeared to dismiss her without noticeable regret, but it did nothing for her

sense of relief when he added derisively, 'Perhaps we'd
be wiser to postpone our little chat yet again, as I'll
have more time later.'

'Oh!' Her eyes widened apprehensively.

Scott laughed dryly. 'You didn't think you were
going to escape, did you?'

CHAPTER SEVEN

THE evening dragged interminably. If she had had her own transport, Sherry would have gone home at midnight, but it was two hours later before Scott said goodbye to the last of his guests and they set out for Googon.

'I'm sure I could have got a lift,' Sherry protested, 'and saved you all this trouble.'

'They were all going the wrong way,' he pointed out reasonably, 'and it's no trouble.'

He didn't hurry. Sherry could have screamed as her nerves grew tighter and she suspected he was deliberately provoking the feeling of tension between them. When at last they reached Googon she breathed a sigh of relief which turned to alarm as she realised she was trapped in the car. The doors were electrically operated and he wouldn't let her out.

'I want a few answers to some simple questions first,' he said, before she could launch an appeal. 'I realise you must be tired, but there's nothing that should tax you unduly.'

His mild sarcasm wasn't reassuring and she looked away from him mutinously. Didn't he think he had done enough damage for one evening? The attention he had paid her at Coomarlee, which she had been unable to explain wasn't what it appeared to be, had evoked embarrassing remarks. If Scott had remained arrogantly indifferent to anything he might have overheard, Sherry had found it exhausting, parrying the supposedly discreet curiosity of his friends.

'I don't think we've anything to talk about,' she muttered fiercely.

Putting a hand under her chin, he turned the pale

114

oval of her face towards him. 'That's better. I like to see your face when I'm talking to you. Now, where was I? Ah, yes, your trip to Bourke. You do get around!'

'So what?' she retorted rudely. 'Can't a girl go anywhere, these days, without arousing curiosity?'

'Not in this case,' he replied adamantly, his eyes narrowing at her tone. 'When I left you yesterday, you were dead beat and without transport. So what do you do? You borrow a car which is barely fit to use on the station and set out on a pleasure trip, because—how did you put it?—you couldn't settle at home.'

'I . . .' she licked dry lips with the tip of her tongue, but stopped as she saw him watching with interest. 'I wanted to see if I could find Kim,' she improvised hastily, wondering why she hadn't thought of it before.

Scott considered this for another narrow-eyed moment before appearing to accept it. 'You almost crashed into Dulcie.'

Sherry shrank from his returning anger. 'She was coming out of your section . . .'

'It doesn't matter what she was doing, Sherry. Don't you realise, if that matchbox contraption of Sam's really hit a vehicle as substantial as the one Dulcie was driving, it would fold up like a concertina!'

Thoroughly confused, Sherry exclaimed, 'I was taking care. Whose side are you on, anyway?'

'I'm not apportioning the blame,' he said severely, 'I'm merely advising caution, in future.' He paused, frowning, searching her face, the fragile, faintly aristocratic features, the straight nose, unsmiling mouth, brilliant blue eyes. 'Was it my invitation that drove you to Bourke? Were you really looking for a new dress?'

Once again she veered round the truth. 'I could do with one!'

Scott's mouth thinned. 'I'm not accusing you of extravagance. Certain things don't add up, that's all. You might have let Dulcie put you off, but there's more than one place in Bourke where you could have bought a dress. There again, after everything that's happened, I believe a new evening gown would have been the last thing on your mind.'

Why did she never allow for Scott's astuteness? 'Maybe I overreacted to the situation, owing to the number of shocks I'd had?'

He studied her veiled, shadowed eyes. 'I wonder?'

Sherry felt the blood drain from her cheeks and the tensing of her stomach muscles made her feel ill. Why was Scott bothering about what she had been doing in Bourke? He had talked of revenge, but surely that didn't include following her movements every minute of the day? Kim had gone for good—as soon as she had seen Dan Cleary and got everything sorted out, she would tell Scott so. Surely seeing her struggle to keep Googon viable would be revenge enough?

'Is the inquisition over, Mr Brady?' she asked.

'Scott!' he commanded tersely.

'I don't have to.'

Suddenly he seemed to come alive to the cool defiance of her tone and his mood swung savagely to taunt her. 'I could make you.'

'How?' she asked recklessly, allowing herself to be goaded.

He laughed. 'You're like a small volcano, aren't you? Always in a constant state of eruption. Come here!'

Terror shivered along her skin. Her breath was rapid, aching in her lungs. 'No!'

He silenced her protest with a hard punishing kiss. Though she struggled against the imprisoning arms that slid round her, she made no more impression than a leaf fighting for survival in a whirlpool. Her eyes closed as his lips sought the warmth of her mouth and a hot, intolerable weakness swept through her. She felt so tired it was easier to give in than resist. Finding Scott's kisses disturbing but not objectionable, it was no great punishment having to endure them. She was only worried that in his arms she might relax her guard and find herself confessing how much she was coming to care for him. Alarmed that this might happen, Sherry fought the inertia that gripped her and renewed her efforts to escape.

He was too close, however, and she had reckoned without his expertise. As he felt her resistance, as if mocking it, the pressure of his mouth increased and she soon discovered how weak and puny was her mind compared to the overriding desires of her body. As his mouth bruised with violence, she became lost to sensation, her lethargy disappearing as she became alive and vibrant in his arms. Her own arms slipped round his neck as she arched against him, while he wound his fingers through the tumbled masses of her hair, lifting her head back to allow his lips to blaze a devastating trail of fire along the creamy length of her throat.

It had happened before. The previous night when he had made love to her in the hotel, she had given in to his overwhelming demands. He had rendered her completely defenceless, then showed restraint. Now it must be her turn.

She tried to halt the increasing wildness of her response by putting her hands on his chest and pushing him away. 'Please, Scott,' she moaned, stiffening in resistance.

For a moment he held her against the hard pressure of his body, then as she gasped another entreaty, he let her go. His triumph must be complete, she thought miserably. Not only was she breathing his name over and over again, she was exhibiting an odd reluctance, when it came to it, to leave his arms.

'You'd better go in,' he said curtly, no apparent indication of victory on his hardening features as he turned from her to release the door lock.

'It's almost dawn,' she whispered, staring at the glow of light pushing over the horizon. The morning was suddenly alive with bird-song bursting into the breathless stillness. Sherry lifted her face to it as she got out the car, feeling the dampness of tears on her cheeks.

'Come along,' Scott said almost roughly, escorting her to the house. 'You should be able to get a few hours' sleep before you have to get up.'

Going inside, she closed the door. She didn't say goodnight or listen for him leaving, though she supposed he must have done. She got exactly two hours' sleep before her alarm went off, having been prudent enough to set it. When she woke she had an ache somewhere, but she hadn't time to locate it before starting breakfast. There was the day's work to discuss with Sam, along with other things. There was too much to do without having to worry about what was happening to her heart.

While Sam was eating breakfast, she asked for another loan of his runabout. She recalled Scott's warning, but what else could she do? She returned Sam's enquiring glance with some impatience. 'I told you I had to see Dan Cleary.'

Sam slowly shook his head. 'I think you must have damaged something yesterday, Sherry. I can't rightly figure it out, but she won't even start, this morning.'

'Won't start?'

'That's right.' Ignoring her wide-eyed dismay, Sam went on stoically eating lamb chops. 'It's probably not much, but none of us has any time to investigate the trouble right now.'

Sherry stared at him, feeling somehow suspicious. 'Your car mightn't be in the same class as a Rolls, Sam, but I'd say she wasn't far behind in performance.'

Sam looked embarrassed and kept his eyes on his breakfast. 'We all get hiccups occasionally.'

After he had gone, she fumed impotently. There was so much to do here and she had to get to Bourke. Getting to Bourke was marginally the more important, and if she had no transport she must try and get a lift.

She would ride as far as the main road and chance her luck.

It was nine o'clock when Sherry unsaddled her horse at the junction and sent her home. The road to Bourke stretched endlessly and she had to grit her teeth to keep going. She could see no sign of anything that looked remotely like a lift. There were plenty of flies and the odd kangaroo, but that was all. As soon as she could, she vowed angrily, she would write and tell Kim exactly what she thought of him! And whether they could afford it or not, while she was in Bourke she would see about another truck! She had been crazy to imagine she could manage without one.

She reckoned she must have covered several miles when Scott turned up. He approached from the opposite direction and stopped when she was level. His face was tight, his eyes icy. He had the look of a man sorely tried.

'What the devil are you up to now?' he snapped.

The sight of him, shirt open at the neck, exposing a lot of his powerful, hair-covered chest, made her already pounding heart race and also increased her temper.

'Mr Brady!' she exclaimed, her small face scarlet. 'One of the reasons I love Australia is because it's always seemed to offer more freedom than any other place, but now I'm not so sure, with you always sitting on my back!'

'Don't be so damned stupid!'

'That as well!' she cried furiously. 'Just because my brother got foolishly involved with your sister, I've no brains either!'

'Sherry!' Scott's voice indicated he was rapidly coming to the end of his patience. 'If you don't shut up and calm down I'll lay you over my knee. Where the hell are you going?'

Not to be outdone, she cried, 'Mind your own damned business!'

'No hope,' he rasped. 'You're going to Bourke.'

'Is there anywhere else,' she snapped back, 'in this godforsaken land? Oh, no!' she almost wept, 'I didn't mean that. Yes, I am going to Bourke, and you can't stop me!'

'No, but I can take you.'

'You must have noticed,' she retorted sarcastically, 'you're going the wrong way.'

'I was looking for strays,' he replied coolly. 'It seems I've found one. Now get in!'

'Thank you, I'd rather not,' she refused, beginning to walk on.

'My God!' He was out of the car so fast she had to gasp. 'Sherry!' he thundered.

His fury should have stopped her in her tracks, but she didn't even pause. She hadn't dreamt he would so swiftly overtake her and snatch her up in his arms. He held her so tightly she was half suffocating against his chest when he threw her into the car.

'Sit there!' he barked. 'Don't dare move.'

Oddly enough, despite her former bravado, Sherry obeyed apprehensively. He crashed down beside her and she was lost in the furious glitter of his eyes. Her sheer indignation didn't escape him, but he took no notice. He seemed more interested in her appearance. His glance was insolent, perhaps to punish her, as it roamed over her body. He didn't miss her heaving breast, her tumbled hair, the wild anger in her face.

'One of these days . . .!' he gritted.

She didn't let him finish. 'I know, you'll strangle me. An eye for an eye . . .'

'That's not my way,' he retorted icily.

'Maybe not,' she replied. 'I didn't think you'd stoop to anything as human as revenge, but I feel you'd like to do something.'

'I'm human enough to have considered it,' he ground out, his hands digging into her shoulders.

'I don't doubt,' she shot back contrarily. 'But you'll

probably settle for showing Googon a lack of neighbourly consideration. From now on, you'll ignore us, especially me.'

'So that is what I'm doing right now, is it?' he asked acidly. 'Inviting you to dinner last night was another form of pretending you don't exist?'

'That was making a convenience of me, remember? You were one short.'

'Well, taking you to Bourke could hardly be called making a convenience of you,' he remarked dry.

'Miss Easten wouldn't like it.'

He released a cool, deep breath; Sherry felt it feathering her face. 'Leave Miss Easten to me.'

'You're welcome!'

He looked as though he would have liked to annihilate her on the spot, but instead he released her with a muttered expletive, turned the car and drove on.

The next few miles were completed in grim silence. Sherry wondered if Scott was going to speak again. He was angry. He was a man who always regarded women with indulgence but some contempt. This didn't mean he didn't want them in his life—he would consider they had their uses—certainly in bed, as long as they were submissive and didn't answer back. Sherry didn't need to be told he thought her manners deplorable and that he was probably thinking of new ways of making her suffer. He might be triumphant if he knew how much she was suffering already. She believed she was falling in love with him. It was something which had taken possession of her so swiftly she had been able to do little about it. His dark image was imposing on her mind night and day, making her restless and unhappy. Whatever obstacles life put in her way, she might get over them, but she didn't think she would ever get over loving Scott Brady.

She was startled when he asked mildly, 'Aren't you going to tell me why you're going to Bourke again, so soon? You know your brother isn't there.'

Cautiously she decided to tell him so much. 'I'd like to buy another truck. We can't manage without one.'

He nodded. 'I understand your problem, if not your panic. Let me loan you something, until Kim returns.'

Sherry was surprised by his offer—and tempted, but she had to refuse. If she accepted a truck from Scott, he could accuse her of borrowing it under false pretences when he learnt Kim wasn't coming back.

'I'd rather not,' she faltered.

He said impatiently, 'I'm not too proud to borrow from my neighbours and I expect them to borrow from me.'

'I'd still rather not,' she insisted, adding awkwardly, 'I appreciate your offer, but I think I'd be wiser to have something of my own.'

They roared into Bourke with Sherry wondering hollowly if she would ever please him. After parking, Scott said curtly, 'I've some business I can attend to, now I'm here. Can you fill in an hour until I'm through, then we can visit a few garages together. You can't know much about buying trucks, so I think you'd be wise to accept my help in this instance, Sherry.'

Unable to dispute it, she agreed. If Dan Cleary and the bank manager gave her the go-ahead, she wouldn't have unlimited funds, so she might need all the help she could get.

That Scott would be engaged for the next hour couldn't have suited her better. She watched him striding along the street before diving into Dan Cleary's office.

Dan Cleary was a middle-aged man, who admired Sherry's spirit even if he couldn't applaud her intentions. 'I've been aware for some time that your brother has no aptitude for farming,' he said, 'but he might have been wiser to have sold up before he went.' Dan didn't know, or pretended he didn't, why Kim had left in such a hurry, but he did add, 'I could have got him a buyer in five minutes, if he'd waited.'

Sherry didn't doubt it, nor did she ask names. She had a good idea!

'I must try and carry on for at least a year,' she said.

'If you didn't have Sam Duffy I couldn't have advised it,' he grunted.

About the truck, he was even more discouraging. 'You're mortgaged up to the hilt and I don't think there'll be much spare cash.'

'It must be a necessary expense, Mr Cleary.'

He gave in with a sigh. 'Then you'd better see Nick Wallace, at the bank.'

The bank manager did say she might have a truck, but was no more enthusiastic about her taking over Googon than Dan Cleary had been.

'Kim hasn't exactly made a go of things, Sherry. And because your late grandfather was an old and valued client, I've gone out of my way to give him all the help I could. Do you think your grandfather would have approved of him going off and leaving Googon to a girl of your age?'

'I'm almost twenty, Mr Wallace,' she replied tersely, getting very tired of everyone doubting her ability. 'Grandfather taught me a lot, and I have to try.'

'I admire your spirit,' he said out aloud what Dan Cleary had merely thought, 'yes, I do.' He looked at her keenly. 'I knew your mother, you know. We grew up together—contemporaries, you might say. She used to write to me occasionally, after she married.'

'Mummy wrote to you?'

'Well,' he cleared his throat slightly as Sherry's voice faltered, 'we were old friends. When your grandfather didn't reply to her letters, she came to rely on me for news of him. It had nothing to do with my position in the bank, of course. She was only interested in his health, and how he was getting on.'

'You—you met my father?'

'Not here. I did on a trip to England. You and your

brother were away at school and I stayed with your parents for a few days.'

Sherry felt stunned. All this and she had never known! 'I wish you'd told me before now,' she whispered. 'I realised Mummy must have had friends, but I never seemed to meet them.'

'Most of them are living elsewhere,' he said ruefully. 'And in time people forget.'

Sherry suspected he hadn't and smiled at him gratefully. 'Thank you for telling me anyway.'

She did get permission to buy a truck, but with a limit set to what she could spend. When she met Scott and she told him how much, he frowned but didn't comment. She had to admit, afterwards, that she might have fared badly if he hadn't been with her as she'd no idea what a good second-hand truck could cost. It could only have been with his help that she managed to get something roadworthy at a reasonable price.

He asked her to have lunch with him while the garage checked it out, and, after the time he had spent, Sherry felt she couldn't very well refuse. He took her to a pleasant hotel, but she didn't feel hungry and merely pushed the food round on her plate. Not being able to tell him about Kim was weighing on her mind, but she felt, at the moment, she couldn't bear a further volley of Scott's disparaging remarks which would surely follow such a confession.

If he noticed her lack of appetite he didn't say anything, and as soon as they finished coffee he took her back to the garage and waited while she collected the truck.

'I'll follow you home,' he said.

'There's no need,' she protested.

'Don't argue!' he returned tightly.

As she met his cooling grey eyes and recognised his usual disapproval of opposition, Sherry gave in helplessly. 'Just as you like,' she agreed, trying not to sound defeated but failing miserably.

She was conscious of him behind her all the way to Googon, and although it should have made her feel better that he was eating her dust, she felt no particular triumph. She wished he would go back to Coomarlee and leave her alone. There was so much to do and she couldn't see herself getting through the half of it if Scott was continually distracting her. On the face of it he was being helpful, but she was suspicious of his kindness. He had made so many threats over the past weeks, she couldn't believe he hadn't meant them. There were different forms of revenge, or different ways of extracting it. If she had been a man, Scott could have knocked her down, but because she was a girl he mightn't find it so simple. Perhaps he was considering attacking her through her emotions, extending his friendship and assistance until she came to rely on him, then withdrawing aloofly, leaving her devastated.

On reaching the homestead, she felt a sense of frustration when he nodded when she offered him a drink. She had thought she had made it plain that she appreciated his help but not his company, and he wasn't a man normally slow on the uptake.

'I'd rather have tea,' he said, when she had hoped he would settle for something quicker, like whisky or beer.

'Very well,' she said stiffly. 'If you go into the lounge I'll not be long.'

He followed her to the kitchen and judging from the determined expression on his face, Sherry guessed she'd be wasting her breath if she repeated her request that he went elsewhere.

Silently she cursed. The stove was out and it would take time to light, and she didn't relish doing it with Scott standing over her, watching every movement. She found an armful of logs and threw them on. The fire roared and within minutes the kitchen was like a furnace. Scott leant against the table, powerful arms folded, grimly eyeing the stove. Sherry tried to stay calm as his cold glance occasionally encompassed her. She fretted as the kettle took ages in boiling.

He startled her by asking curtly, 'Have you found anyone to stay with you at night, until Kim returns?'

Again she missed a chance of telling him the truth. She excused herself this time by telling herself she must speak to Sam first. 'I'll ask one of the Aborigine girls to stay,' she replied briefly.

'I'll have a word with Sam before I go, to make sure you do,' he said coolly.

This rankled. 'I'd rather you didn't. You aren't responsible for what happens here, and after all your talk of revenge, wouldn't it suit you very well if someone murdered me in my bed? Then,' she added for good measure, 'you might have no trouble getting your hands on Googon!'

Grey eyes glittering, Scott rasped, 'So that's what you think?'

Sherry stared back at him doubtfully. 'Are you denying you would like to?'

Irritably he replied. 'I don't deny I would try and buy Googon, if it ever came on the market, but I certainly wouldn't be party to anything underhand, as you appear to be suggesting.'

Sherry frowned. 'I thought perhaps that was why you were helping me, after being so—so unfriendly.'

His mouth twisted ironically. 'I see.' Frowning for a moment, he said, 'After I left you this morning, I did some thinking. Knowing Ellen, I have to admit she might be as much at fault as Kim. I still believe your brother acted deplorably, Sherry, but my sister must be partly responsible for Kim being away. So perhaps that's why I feel morally obliged to do what I can for you until he gets back. It's probably too late to talk of reprisals anyway.'

Sherry lowered her eyes to hide the dawning dismay in them. What would Scott say if she confessed that Kim might not have been away if he hadn't had the

chance of a new start in England? Ellen was certainly
guilty of deceiving her brother, but she wasn't really
responsible for Kim leaving Googon. However, if Scott
knew that, he might wash his hands of Sherry Grant
altogether. It was tempting not to tell him, to go on
allowing him to feel she had been wronged by his
family, so that she might bask in his protective care for
at least a little longer. Sam wouldn't betray her, and
though Dan Cleary and Nick Wallace both knew the
truth about Kim, they were unlikely to say anything.

Deciding impulsively not to enlighten Scott for a few
more days bothered Sherry's conscience, but she tried
to soothe it by reminding herself that he owed her
something for treating her so roughly. As long as she
didn't take his offers of help too seriously. She might
have fallen in love with him, but she must remember it
was Dulcie Easten whom he was going to marry. Or if it
wasn't Dulcie, it would be another girl like her, with an
impeccable background.

She felt Scott raising her chin with a thoughtful
finger. 'Are you very worried about your brother?' he
asked grimly. 'Shall I make some enquiries? I don't
suppose he's gone far.'

'No!' Sherry refused quickly, her cheeks flushed, 'I
expect he—he knows what he's doing.'

Scott looked as if he was going to say more then
changed his mind. 'I'm sure he'll be back before anyone
notices.'

Sherry sighed, her duplicity weighing heavier than she
had thought it would. 'No one seemed aware of anything
amiss last night. I scarcely heard Ellen's name mentioned.'

Scott's mouth tightened. 'It was assumed she was
away, but there'll be an announcement in the
newspapers tomorrow.'

'So you aren't going to just ignore her marriage?'
Sherry's blue eyes brightened.

'No, but I don't want to discuss it,' he replied
repressively.

Sherry realised this. The attempts she had made the other morning had met with grim silence. She liked Ellen, she wasn't snobbish, the way Dulcie Easten was. Scott was sure his sister would never make a poor man's wife, but he might be proved wrong.

'Ellen's marriage——' she began, forgetting Scott's warning.

'Enough!' he snapped, once again dictatorial.

Unhappily resentful at being spoken to so abruptly, Sherry grasped the hot kettle handle and let go of it with a gasp of pain.

'My God!' Scott swooped as the kettle clattered on the stove and she jumped back in fright. 'What have you done now? You aren't capable of running a kitchen, let alone a station!'

'I'm all right!' she grasped her scorched hand, glaring at him as he grabbed it forcefully, 'I wasn't thinking what I was doing!'

'You should have been,' he said harshly. 'You get on a lot better if you concentrate on your own problems and not on those that belong to people who don't consider yours!'

'Oh, you aren't human!' she cried as he wrenched her small, clenched hand open to expose the seared skin. Her hand felt numb. There was more feeling shooting up her arm from the clasp of Scott's fingers than from the burn.

'Under the tap with you,' he ordered grimly, turning the kitchen one full on. The water trickled, then splashed, almost drowning them. 'Talk about inadequate plumbing!' he said savagely. 'Your whole kitchen needs refitting. It's a pity neither your grandfather or brother ever heard of modernisation!'

The cold water and his clipped tones were certainly easing the discomfort of her palm if not her mind. And Scott's administrations were amazingly gentle, once she stopped struggling.

'I—I like the kitchen as it is,' she muttered, trying not

to be conscious of his hard chest pressed against her back as, with his arms round her, he held her still. 'Modern kitchens are soulless.'

'But less dangerous.' His breath was on her cheek as he bent to inspect her hand more closely, and she began to tremble.

He frowned, feeling the tension in her slight body tight against him. 'Is it hurting badly?'

'No,' she confessed, 'not now. I think I got a fright more than anything else.'

Scott nodded. 'There's quite a bit of redness, all the same. Where do you keep your medicine chest?'

She told him, at the back of the house, and when he returned with it she stared at the top of his dark head as he dressed her hand. Her heart was beating restlessly and she felt suddenly frightened of her own reactions. Such an intensity of feeling was whirling through her that she hoped feverishly Scott would never kiss her again for she feared, if he did, she might respond so violently she might betray how much she loved him and be ashamed of herself for ever.

Scott glanced up, frowning. 'I've seen worse. A bandage should keep it comfortable and prevent more damage, but it should be all right by tomorrow.'

Sherry wasn't even listening. She was gazing at him, her eyes again trapped by something in his she found impossible to escape. Her colour drained as she realised his hold over her and when a log fell from the stove, breaking the trance she was in, she almost cried with relief.

'Thank you,' she said huskily, her eyes now on her bandaged hand. 'I'll make your tea.'

'Never mind that,' a muscle twitched in his cheek, 'I'll make it. You sit down.'

She groped towards a kitchen chair, but he turned her in the direction of the veranda. 'Out there,' he said curtly. 'It's too hot in here. I'll be with you in a minute.'

Sherry saw Sam after dinner. She knew, in all

fairness, she had to talk to him. She felt freer, since having been to Bourke, to tell him that Ellen Brady had married Barry White's overseer and that Kim had left Australia and returned to England. She didn't say he wasn't coming back, because she couldn't be sure of that.

Sam didn't appear surprised by what she told him, making Sherry wonder wryly if he might have known more all along than he had ever let on? He assured her again that she could rely on him and she wasn't to worry. He and the men would see her through.

Scott hadn't stayed long after drinking his tea. He had left abruptly after advising her to take care of her hand and to think about some alterations in the kitchen.

'I have some meetings in Melbourne I have to go to,' he told her, 'and I want to see Barry White. I'll be gone several days, perhaps a week, but I'll give you a ring when I return.'

He hadn't given her time to say it wasn't necessary, having taken himself off with a casual word of farewell. He left her staring after him, engulfed by a peculiar sense of loss, which she would rather not have felt.

By the time the shearers arrived, Sherry had made arrangements with Sam which she thought would suit them both. Because she felt she must be straight with him, she had confessed that she had no idea what Kim's plans might be at the end of a year. She knew that this would depend on his success with Harold Gibson. She couldn't even promise, despite what Kim had said in his letter, that he wouldn't sell before the year was out, but Sam had been more than willing to take things a day at a time. Suspecting that he was hoping that if Googon was sold the new owner might keep him on, Sherry resolved, if this ever happened, she would do her utmost to ensure that Sam's job was safe.

The more Sherry thought about it, the higher were her hopes that Kim wouldn't sell Googon. If she could

run it and make a profit from it, it might suit him better
to have something in the background, if all else failed.

In this frame of mind, she was determined to make a
success of things and made sure everything was ready
for the shearers when they arrived. Her hand, as Scott
had predicted, was none the worse, apart from a little
tenderness, next morning, and she rode out with the
men to help with the last of the mustering. They had
enough horses, but she envied Jamie and some of the
others their trail bikes, that could move the stock far
quicker than she and Sam could. Even more, she envied
Scott his helicopters which could coax even the most
wily sheep from the low scrub. He used them chiefly,
she knew, on cattle on a property he had over the
border, in Queensland. Sam called the men who flew
them airborne cowboys, but she guessed he sometimes
wished they had something of the kind here. It wasn't
much fun herding mobs of stubborn sheep in searing
heat especially when—it seemed clear to Sherry—they
would rather stay where they were.

CHAPTER EIGHT

YET, for all the rigours and drawbacks of outback life, Sherry loved it. Despite the minimal rainfall, searing temperatures and frequent dust storms, she had no real fault to find with it. The wide plains of what was commonly referred to as Back o' Bourke were rough, wild and inhospitable, but there was so much beauty too—the drought-dried river beds, the white ghostgums, the creeks lined with coolabah and sandlewood which somehow managed to survive the fiercest bush fires. Even the twisting wind devils that could scour an area, she found fascinating. The landscape had a sinister beauty. To a visitor it might often appear alien and strange, but for the farmer and grazier, for whom it was home, it represented a way of life few would exchange for any other.

The holding yards next to the shearing sheds were full of mobs of sheep when the shearing contractor turned up. He had his usual number of men, but unfortunately no cook. Sherry listened in dismay to Sam when he came from their quarters.

'Seems like he took sick yesterday, Miss Sherry, an' they had to fly him into town. Doc suspects something's wrong, but it could be a day or two before he's sure. Real crook, he is, they say.'

Sherry knew crook meant sick, and it wasn't a word the average Australian used lightly. All the same, she frowned. 'Surely they could have found another cook?'

'Seems not,' Sam looked uncomfortable, 'and they didn't want to wait, not when we wus expecting them. Do you think you could do the job, Miss Sherry?'

While they both knew her grandfather would never have approved, Sherry felt she couldn't refuse. She cooked for the shearers and it proved very hot and tiring. The facilities for cooking at the shearers' quarters were no better than those at the house and with only the help of Leda, the little Aborigine girl, who stayed with her at nights, she struggled to feed numerous men who seemed possessed of enormous appetites. She had little time to watch the actual clipping, although she did manage once or twice to get down to the big sheds to see how swiftly the shearers could remove a sheep's fleece.

By evening she was usually exhausted, but always next morning she was up early, refreshed, ready for another day. Her own vitality surprised her and she didn't really mind being extra busy as it didn't leave her much time to think of Scott. She hadn't decided yet how she was going to tell him about Kim, and the longer she put off the more difficult it was going to be. If he heard the true story from someone else, she could imagine his anger. Rather than think of it, she concentrated on other things.

The shearers, Sam said, should be through by the end of the week. Sam was working hard as well, supervising the grading and packing of the wool, while Jamie and the other station hands saw to getting the shorn sheep back to the paddocks again. They would all be tired by the end of the week, but this would be just one more job completed before they started on another.

On Thursday evening, Sherry and Leda began stacking dishes after pouring out what seemed like gallons of tea and coffee for the shearing team. The men had just eaten a huge meal and were relaxed as they talked and joked. Bob McKenzie, the contract boss, was making sure the conversation didn't become ribald, so as not to offend the two girls, but he needn't have worried, for the men liked Sherry and had a great respect for her. They knew her from the previous years, when she had followed her grandfather round the sheds, showing a great interest in what they were doing.

Someone got out his guitar and began to strum until Bob called for Waltzing Matilda and they all started singing. Leda nudged Sherry and they stopped washing up to listen.

Waltzing Matilda was Australia's national folk song and was famous throughout the world. The lyrics for it had been written about eighty years ago by A. B. 'Banjo' Paterson, while visiting a cattle station in Queensland. Sherry wondered if many other songs would ever be quite so well known.

She and Leda not only listened, they joined in the chorus, and when it was finished, Sherry impulsively asked one of the men, whom she knew only as Will, if he still remembered Clancy of the Overflow, one of Paterson's other ballads, which she had happened to hear him reciting the year before. Much to her delight he said he did and amidst cheers and a few catcalls from the others, he stood up, bowed to Sherry and began.

'He was shearing when I knew him, so I sent a letter to him,
    Just on spec, addressed as follows, "Clancy, of The Overflow."
    And the answer came directed in a writing unexpected (And I think the same was written with a thumb nail dipped in tar);
    'Twas his shearing mates who wrote it, and verbatim I will quote it,
    "Clancy's gone to Queensland droving, and we don't know where he are".
    In my wild erratic fancy visions come to me of Clancy gone a-droving down the Cooper where the Western drovers go,
    As the stock are slowly stringing, Clancy rides behind them singing,
    For the drover's life has pleasures that the townsfolk never know.'

Will had a good voice for poetry and Sherry was

disappointed when he stopped abruptly. Thinking he
had forgotten the rest, she was just about to beg him to
continue when she realised everyone was looking at
something behind her. With a start she swung round to
find Scott standing in the doorway.

He nodded to the men without altering the grimness
of his face, but it was to Sherry he spoke. 'Could I have
a word with you?'

The men were finished, anyway. They disappeared,
leaving her alone with him. Leda went too. Sherry felt
deserted and unfairly, she thought, loaded with a sense
of guilt. As Scott's glacial glance again toured the
makeshift kitchen, she was even more disconcerted to
hear herself stammering awkwardly.

'S-someone had to do it. Their cook is ill.'

Scott's eyes swung back to her, pinning her
disapprovingly. 'I could have supplied half a dozen
cooks. All you had to do was ring.'

'You were away.'

'I left instructions that you were to have all the help
you required.'

She stared at his rigid features. 'But that's ridiculous,'
she retorted. 'I know you offered assistance, but I
imagined you'd set limits?'

His eyes darkened. 'Could we go to the house?' he
asked politely. 'We can't talk here.'

All her protective hackles said no. She glanced at the
sink wildly. 'I have these dishes to finish and breakfast
to set.'

'Leave it.' His mouth compressed as he almost swept
her outside. When she stumbled he merely picked her
up and walked on without pausing. 'I'll have a new
cook here first thing in the morning. He'll deal with all
that.'

Sherry tried to free herself, but his arms held her fast.
She was ashamed that she didn't struggle harder, but
either tiredness or the feeling of his heart beating
strongly against hers caused all her strength to leave

her. It was dark, she comforted herself, when Scott
clearly showed no intention of putting her down. No
one would see.

Scott bent his head, freezing her with an oppressive
glance, making sure she didn't argue. Their eyes
caught and held and the sudden contact made all her
pulses race. The body warmth between them was
making her languorous, she began to feel she was
floating. She watched the hard line of his face
achingly, unaware of how much of herself she was
revealing.

His footsteps halted under the shadow of a tree that
enclosed them in secret scents and privacy. What now?
she wondered, resting her cheek weakly against his
shoulder. If he put her down she might faint, so
overwhelming were the emotions rushing through her.

He didn't put her down—if anything his arms
tightened. His hand tugged at her hair, pulling back her
head, and his mouth slowly touched her lips, brushing
them so lightly it was merely a feather-like sensation on
her skin. She felt her lips part and violent feelings, such
as she had never known before, wrenched through her.
Suddenly she wanted Scott to crush her. She didn't
want mercy or tenderness, she wanted his ruthlessness
and passion.

His lips hardened as he felt the explosive desire
between them, and for a moment, as her mouth
shuddered open beneath his and her arms wound fast
about his neck, he didn't spare her. It wasn't until she
winced that he set her down.

Sherry was shattered and trembling. Had she really
asked for that? Scott's voice mocked her.

'Until you learn to recognise what you're inviting,
you'd better stop playing games.'

She must have swayed, because although he didn't
take hold of her again, he grasped her arm. 'Come on,'
he said curtly. 'We were on our way somewhere,
remember?'

Leda had reached the house before them. Scott told her to run along home and come back in an hour. As the girl obeyed without a murmur, Sherry's indignation returned in a rush.

'You aren't at Coomarlee now, you know! You can't act like a dictator here, ordering people about. I don't know what the shearers will think!'

'They're a decent bunch of men,' he retorted coldly. 'Strange as it may seem to you, they might even approve of my intervention. Someone has to look after you. Where was Sam?'

'He left only minutes before you arrived,' she replied sullenly.

'He shouldn't have,' Scott said firmly. 'I'll have a word with him.'

Sherry bristled, resenting his high-handedness, even though she loved him. As soon as he had appeared, the shearers had gone, melting away like the snowflakes she'd almost forgotten about. They hadn't looked like frightened men, just very obliging ones, and she could guess why. They sheared for Scott, too, which would be much more lucrative than the amount they collected from Googon. Whereas at Googon, they kept mostly the Peppin Merino, which accounted for the great bulk of the national clip, Scott, especially on his more southern properties, ran predominantly the very fine wooled Saxon Merino, whose wool brought the highest prices. Which probably meant the shearers got higher percentages.

'I'd rather you didn't interfere,' she said tersely, trying not to allow her eyes to dispute her anger by feasting on him as if she hadn't seen him for a year instead of a mere week. 'I'm old enough to take care of myself and I can do what I like.'

'Would your brother have let you be shearers' cook?' he asked mildly.

Sherry flushed. 'He—well, no, he mightn't have, but it—it's nothing to be ashamed of!'

'All the same,' Scott looked at her adamantly, 'you won't do it again.'

Sherry couldn't let it go. 'All right,' she glared at him from indignant blue eyes, 'so you send over a cook. Have you ever thought of what people might say?'

'Why should anyone say anything?' he snapped.

Knowing she deserved the mocking censure in his voice, the pink in Sherry's cheeks deepened. It was unlikely that anyone would connect their names, either romantically or otherwise. He was only emphasising what he had told her before, that socially they were so far apart it would be ludicrous.

'I'm sorry,' she sighed unhappily.

He sighed, a hard sound, his eyes boring into the back of her suddenly bent head. 'What was going on down at the sheds, anyway?'

'Just a bit of a sing-song. I was enjoying it.'

'You're better out of it,' he said abruptly. 'In a situation like that, men can easily forget women are present. Your ears could soon have been burning.'

She felt they might argue over it all night! 'Did you come for anything special?' she asked quickly. 'You did say you wanted to speak to me.'

The mocking glint in his eyes betrayed that he saw through her tentative attempt to divert him. 'I did,' he nodded coolly. 'I wanted to hear how you were surviving. I presume your brother is still hiding out?'

Sherry stiffened. 'Yes.'

'Haven't you any idea where he is, so you can tell him it's not necessary?'

All Sherry's old fears of Scott's anger, whether for Kim or herself, converged on her, making the truth something still impossible to confess. 'He's sure to be back,' she muttered indistinctly.

'He's taking his time.'

In panicky haste, she offered Scott a drink, with over-profuse apologies for keeping him standing around without anything.

He heard her out patiently, his eyes slightly narrowed. 'I wouldn't mind—if you'll join me?'

She glanced down at her sticky hands, her clothing, damp with perspiration. 'I'm scarcely in a fit state,' she murmured, hoping he would take the hint and leave.

If she was throwing out hints, he wasn't biting. 'Go and have a shower,' he suggested blandly, 'I'll be making coffee while you're busy. At least we can be sure you won't burn yourself again.'

She gazed at him wonderingly. 'You haven't forgotten?'

His eyes narrowed darkly. 'I've been worried about you while I've been away. Apparently not without reason.'

She said quickly, 'Did you have a good trip?'

Wryly, he gave her a firm push. 'Run along.'

After showering hastily, Sherry put on a pair of clean jeans and a shirt. She only took time over her hair, brushing it into a silky cloud. It fell well past her shoulders and she resolved to have it cut at the first opportunity. She didn't bother with make-up, just a touch of lip-gloss that made her skin look whiter and matched the faint blush of pink in her cheeks. It was hot and she daringly opened her shirt a little more. Scott Brady was unlikely to notice if she unbuttoned it all the way to her waist!

He had coffee made, but instead of being in the kitchen she found him in the lounge. He had placed the tray on a small table and was studying the shabby carpet, the cane furniture which, though comfortable, had seen better days.

Sherry paused in the doorway, watching him, drinking in his tall darkness, the strong lines of his powerful body. His kisses, half an hour ago, had shaken her to her very roots, yet he might only need to crook his little finger to have her flying into his arms again.

He glanced up, and meeting the long stare of his cool grey eyes, she felt the familiar spark leap between them.

Slowly he walked towards her. 'You look——' he hesitated, as though the word he had choosen wouldn't do, 'better.'

Firmly leading her to the sofa, he made her sit down while he poured their coffee. She didn't protest but kept her eyes on his hands, focussing blindly on the dark hairs on his wrist. Slowly she lifted her eyes to his face, her glance touching the hard line of his mouth again, incredibly dazed.

He sat down beside her, not saying anything more until they finished their coffee, when he pushed the table away.

'Did you enjoy that?' he asked abruptly.

'Yes, you make very good coffee,' she smiled, unable to remember what it tasted like, but Scott's easier tones loosening her tongue. 'You still haven't told me how you got on in Melbourne.'

'It was hot,' he frowned broodingly, his eyes on her hair. 'The heat was intense, dry and crackling. They're afraid of fire.'

'That bad?' she gazed at him apprehensively. Scott Brady wasn't a man to exaggerate and she knew the disaster bush fires could bring in their wake.

'Probably,' he brushed her fears aside. 'I wasn't there long.'

Sherry bit her lip. 'You were going to see Barry White?' She wouldn't have asked him this, but she was really probing for news of Ellen.

'I saw him,' he replied, his mouth tightening, daring her to ask more.

That was clearly all she was going to get out of him. Scott thought she was being too curious. Sherry sighed, moving restlessly.

'Do you still not want me to make enquiries regarding your brother?' he asked, bending anxiously towards her.

It was his query, not his nearness, that caused her to jump to her feet like a startled fawn. She didn't want to

discuss Kim, but she didn't want Scott to know she
didn't; she was still too unsure of the situation to tell
him anything. 'I wish you'd m-mind your own
business!' she cried without thinking.

'Okay,' he was standing beside her before she'd
realised he'd moved, his face a hard, dark mask. 'Don't
alarm yourself, Sherry. That's one of the easiest things
to do. I can oblige immediately.'

'Oh, please!' as she realised he was furious, anguish
darkened her eyes. 'I'm sorry.'

'You didn't mean it?'

His curtness made her hesitate as it somehow aroused
her own anger again. Instead of shaking her head, she
heard herself snapping wildly, 'Yes, on second
thoughts, I do. At least in some things I wish you
wouldn't interfere.'

He replied coldly. 'In that case it might be better if I
stayed away. Then I won't need to worry over making a
mistake.' He paused, a muscle flexing in his jaw where
the tanned skin stretched taut. 'I'll see you have all the
assistance you need until your brother returns, of
course. I believe in recompense.'

He was at the door before she could collect herself,
because it had all happened so quickly she felt stunned.
One moment they had been talking quietly, the next
quarrelling violently. And now Scott was leaving. She
heard her voice call his name on a high note.

'Stay where you are, Sherry,' he barely glanced over
his shoulder at her distraught face, 'I'll see myself out.'

When he had gone, Sherry collapsed where she was
and burst into tears, wishing suddenly that she was
dead. Scott had left in anger. This time she had
provoked him beyond what he was prepared to put up
with and he wouldn't be coming back. Although she
couldn't bear to think of not seeing him again, when
she was more composed she tried to convince herself it
was just as well. The less she saw of him, the sooner she
might forget him. She had to believe that, or else she

might go insane! Wearily she dragged herself from the
living room and went to bed.

She was dismayed the next morning, on rising early,
to find a new cook already in control. The new cook,
moreover, had orders not to let her even set foot in the
shearers' kitchen. For Sherry Grant this was now out of
bounds.

For an impulsive moment Sherry thought angrily of
telling the man to go back to Coomarlee, or wherever
he came from, but she was frightened of provoking a
scene. Instead she contented herself with a repressive
glance and ran angrily to find Sam. She had to get rid
of the man, and Sam would know how to do it without
causing further offence.

Having counted on Sam's support, she was daunted
when he refused to give it. When she protested that she
could have easily gone on cooking for the shearers, he
refused to agree. Quite curtly, for Sam, he told her he
thought Scott was quite right in sending a man to do it.
He'd had a long talk with Scott, last night, and didn't
want to go against him.

'I shouldn't have asked you to do it in the first place,
Miss Sherry,' he told her. 'Your grandfather wouldn't
have liked it, so I'm backing Mr Brady up, in this,
anyway.'

Shooting Sam a resentful glance, Sherry returned to
the house. She had been tempted to remind him that Mr
Brady wasn't boss here yet! In other circumstances she
mightn't have hesitated, but she knew it wouldn't be
easy to make Sam understand the complications of the
matter without explaining more than she wanted to.

She attended to the stove, making a cup of tea she
didn't want, though she sat down and tried to drink it.
Suddenly she knew she must see Scott and tell him the
truth about Kim. She was accepting Scott's help under
false pretences and had no possible excuse for doing so
any longer. She had put off far too long in any case.
From blaming her for what had happened, Scott was

now blaming Ellen and himself. He believed it was because of Ellen that Kim had left and was staying away. If she didn't tell Scott the whole truth immediately, he might, when he did find out, as he must, despise her even more than he did now.

With a weary glance at her unfinished tea, Sherry pushed the tumbled hair from her eyes and decided she would go to Coomarlee and see him that morning, if he wouldn't come here. Thinking he might prefer to see her here, rather than at his place, she went to give him a ring. He might say no to even seeing her again, on whatever pretext, but at least if he did she would always know she had tried.

She was told, however, on contacting Coomarlee, that Scott was out and wouldn't be home until evening. Recognising Mrs Fox's voice, Sherry asked where he was.

Clearly Mrs Fox resented what Sherry realised was a rather presumptuous question. 'Who is speaking?' she asked stiffly.

'Sherry Grant,' Sherry revealed haltingly.

'I'm afraid I'm unable to divulge Mr Brady's whereabouts,' the woman said coldly.

'Well, would you ask him to give me a ring, as soon as he comes in?' Sherry pleaded.

Despite her humble tones, no one rang. And if Scott had done so she couldn't have missed him, for when she wasn't there herself, she had Leda stationed near the telephone with strict instructions to find her should anyone ring. When, in desperation, she rang Coomarlee again, about nine, she was told Mr Brady didn't wish to be disturbed.

Realising that no amount of meekness was going to get her past Mrs Fox, Sherry hurriedly called to Leda that she had to see someone but wouldn't be late. Without waiting to change the short skirt she was wearing for something more practical, she set out for Coomarlee. The truck was going well, for which she breathed a sigh of relief. She might be acting impetuously, calling on Scott at this hour, but if she didn't see him she knew she could never sleep!

It was almost ten when she reached her destination and when Scott opened the door himself, she guessed his staff had already retired to their own quarters for the night. The expression on his face, as he saw who was standing on his doorstep, wasn't exactly inviting, but he did ask her to come in.

Because he said nothing, apart from those two coldly polite words, she found herself stammering, 'I had to see you . . .'

He must have been working in his study or simply relaxing, for he had discarded his jacket and tie and his shirt was half unbuttoned. To the world he presented a cool, impenetrable mask, but underneath her feminine antennae picked up his sensual vitality.

'Isn't it rather late to come dashing over from Googon?' he asked, as she turned to face him in the hall. 'Why didn't you give me a ring?'

'I did,' she felt a faint heat touch her skin as his eyes went slowly over her, 'I asked Mrs Fox to give you a message.'

'Did you? She must have forgotten,' he replied, without notable rancour. 'Well, now you're here, what can I do for you? Is the cook I sent not satisfactory?'

'It's not that . . .'

'Good. So you're after something else?'

'No!' His cool glance wasn't making things easy for her, but she supposed she couldn't blame him. 'I'm not here to ask for more favours. I wanted to explain about Kim.'

'There's something I don't already know?'

'I think so, yes.'

With what seemed deliberate insolence, his eyes made a return trip over the pronounced curve of her breasts until the colour in her cheeks deepened. 'You'd better come in here, then,' he responded, ushering her through to the lounge and asking her to sit down.

He left her to pour two drinks. 'Actually, I've something to say myself.'

Wondering what it could be, Sherry numbly accepted the brandy he gave her. 'Anything special?' she asked.

'Nothing so special it won't keep. I'll hear you out first. After you've had your drink,' added Scott, so firmly she dared not argue.

Taking a nervous sip of the brandy, she looked anywhere but at him. Scott's house was nice, she thought absently. All the furnishings were good, the colour schemes in the various rooms soothing. That was something she disliked at Googon. The colours of the plains were vivid, even harsh, and sometimes she longed, indoors, for something softer than Googon offered.

'Drink up,' Scott said impatiently, sitting down beside her and touching her arm. 'It will do you good.'

She obeyed, though she wasn't sure it was good for her and it made her choke, but it did warm her blood and give her some courage.

'Scott,' she said slowly, her eyes on her empty glass until he removed it from her hands, 'I'm sorry about last night. It was inexcusable, speaking to you as I did, after you'd been so kind.'

He frowned. 'You didn't come all the way here to tell me that?'

'No,' her voice was unsteady, 'I came to tell you the truth about Kim.'

'The—truth?'

'Yes,' she said quickly, before her courage failed her. 'I should have told you sooner, I really should. I realised, today, I was taking help from you which I'd no right to.'

'Try and be more explicit,' he said curtly.

Sherry realised she was explaining things badly, but it wasn't easy. 'Kim isn't coming back,' she whispered. 'He's returned to England, for good.'

Scott didn't reply immediately and she looked up to

find him staring at her. She thought he was feeling something, but she couldn't be sure what it was. His face was coldly expressionless again.

'You'd better begin at the beginning, hadn't you?' he suggested.

Helplessly she nodded. 'There's not a lot. When I got back to Googon, after we'd been to Brisbane, I found a letter from Kim.'

'So soon?'

'He'd paid someone to deliver it. In it, he said he wasn't coming back; that the whole business with Ellen had been a joke—at least, it had started out that way. As you suspected, he'd done it as a break from boredom and because he imagined you considered him no good.'

Scott's eyes hardened, but he only said, as she hesitated, 'Go on.'

'He had the chance of a fresh start in England and he decided to take it. Unknown to me, someone had been asking him to go back for ages.'

'And you? What's going to happen to you? Did he say?'

Scott's voice was well under control, so why did she sense a kind of violence in him? Nervously, Sherry hesitated, but there seemed nothing else to do but continue. 'He—he asked me to carry on for a year, so that if this London venture fails, he would still have Googon.'

'To come back to or sell?'

'To—to come back to,' she muttered. That wasn't what Kim had implied at all, but it sounded better.

Scott retorted, witheringly astute, 'You're still loyal, aren't you?'

Sherry didn't want to think about it. She couldn't be sure. What she did know was that she hated Scott's disparagement, because it seemed to reflect on her. She didn't reply.

Scott wasn't finished. 'You didn't agree to stay on, I hope?'

She hesitated. 'I haven't heard from Kim since and I haven't got his new address.'

'You must know where you might be able to locate him?'

She nodded uneasily, not wanting to confess that she hadn't felt like it.

With a muttered curse, Scott caught hold of her chin, forcing her face up as though he was determined to read something from it. 'Your brother must be perfectly aware you aren't capable of running Googon on your own.'

'Why not?' She flushed, angry with herself for looking to him for assurance which he wasn't likely to give. 'Sam will help.'

She found it humiliating that Scott didn't even bother to argue. 'How much is your brother paying you for probably killing yourself?' he asked.

'There's no need to be nasty!' she retaliated. 'Kim's always been fair.'

'Is that what you call it?' he jeered. 'Why didn't he take you with him to the U.K.?'

'It wouldn't have been convenient,' she said quickly. 'But you don't have to worry. I realise you think I'd be better out of the way, but I promise not to bother you any more. I came this evening to tell you that. I know I should have told you before, but I thought there might be a chance Kim might change his mind and come back, in spite of what he said in his letter.'

This wasn't the sole reason she hadn't explained everything until now, but she couldn't possibly tell him how she'd been trying to make sure he couldn't get his hands on Googon.

Scott asked, with apparent detachment, 'Who is your brother working for in London?'

'Someone called Harold Gibson. He used to work with my father. I realise your opinion of my father,' she added hastily, but he broke in,

'I was talking to Nick Wallace today.'

'Nick—Wallace?'

'Yes, in Bourke.'

Shock rushed through Sherry. Mr Wallace would surely never have betrayed what financial straits she was in. 'Had it anything to do with me?' she asked cautiously.

'In a way.' Scott let go of her chin but went on looking at her, observing her changing colour. 'Your grandfather's name cropped up. As a matter of fact, Nick was reminiscing, as people are apt to do, about their younger days, and it became clear he had known your mother.'

'You—you asked about her?'

He didn't seem to notice Sherry was having difficulty in speaking. 'I did,' his voice hardened. 'He told me about visiting your parents in London, the kind of business your father was in, the way he lived.'

Sherry was silent, her head bent. Funny how it didn't seem to matter any more. Suddenly that part of her life had little meaning. She could remember it without wishing to return to it. Her roots were here now, not in London.

'You must have been very young when you lost your parents,' Scott said quietly.

'Amost seventeen, not that young.' She looked at him enquiringly. 'Is this what you had to tell me?'

'Yes.' He was staring at her watchfully. Sherry thought dazedly that he might have been considering how much she could take. 'Your brother must have known before he left Googon that your father's name had been cleared. Did he tell you?'

When her head moved in assent, he commented coldly, 'It's a pity he didn't stay in London after the crash, then it might have been sorted out sooner.'

She couldn't dispute this, but she felt it was too late for recriminations. She almost said it might have been better if her grandfather hadn't pressurised Kim, but it seemed pointless. She murmured something about

hindsight which merely earned a contemptuous exclamation.

Scott sounded grim, but she noticed he offered not a
hint of regret for presuming her father had been a
disreputable money-lender. It wouldn't be his way to
apologise for something like that. He had told her what he
had learnt from Nick Wallace, which would, as far as he
was concerned, set the record straight. Nothing had really
changed, of course. He would still commit her socially to
the level he would consider her family had fallen to.

She stared at the carpet, trying to lose herself in its
beautiful mellow colours. His lack of remorse didn't
hurt as much as his remark that Kim should have taken
her with him. He couldn't have made it clearer that he
would be glad to see the last of her!

His voice interrupted her painful thoughts, startling
her afresh. 'You didn't tell me the truth about your
brother as soon as you knew for fear I might try to take
Googon from you. In your twisted little mind you were
so sure I had villainous intentions you had to dash
round consulting other people first, trying to get a
guarantee that I couldn't.'

Sherry caught her breath and went white, her guilt so
plainly showing that a look of scorn crossed his face. It
was too late to protest, but words tumbled out before
she could stop them.

'I never mentioned your name. At least——' her
voice faltered uncertainly as she tried to recall exactly
what she had said to Dan Cleary, 'if I did, I would
certainly not accuse you of being dishonest. And
anything,' she added bitterly, 'that I told Dan Cleary
ought to have been confidential!'

'Dan Cleary told me nothing,' Scott retorted with a
contemptuous smile, the savagery in his tone shrivelling
her as he leant nearer. 'Your opinion of me seems no
secret. You'd like to make me out as a monster with an
insatiable appetite for land. I might just take Googon
and you with it, before I'm finished. Just for revenge.'

CHAPTER NINE

SHERRY froze as blinding shock hit her and she sat motionless, wanting to rush from the room but feeling unable to move. Her face, which had gone white, now flamed with colour, and she began protesting bitterly without being conscious of what she was saying. Scott's threats terrified her, and if he carried them out it wouldn't be rape. She suspected he knew the effect he had on her and with his experience would be able to make her respond until she was practically begging him to make love to her.

She flinched from the contempt in his eyes, but somehow it steadied her, changing her ineffectual babbling into sharper anger. 'You said you weren't interested in revenge any more!'

'So now,' he murmured silkily, 'you're accusing me of lying?'

'Well, aren't you?' she cried.

'This time,' he said menacingly, 'I want to punish you for thinking the worst of me, when you had no reason.'

Sherry shrank back as his eyes flicked coldly over her. 'I wouldn't let you punish me the way you threaten, in the way you implied!'

Scott laughed softly and her senses leapt in alarm as he spoke. 'You couldn't stop me.'

It was what she had feared all along. She stared at him, her lips parted on a frightened gasp. Trying to protest, she found herself mesmerised by molten grey eyes full of smouldering intent. His mouth, when it suddenly covered hers, was something she had no strength to avoid.

The unexpectedness of his action caught Sherry unawares, and before she could collect herself suffici-

ently to struggle, his arms were around her, holding her
fast. When she did try and beat at his chest with her
small fists, the light pressure of his mouth hardened to
hurt her for trying to escape.

Scott's arms were too strong, his kisses too insistent.
Her ability to think coherently was rapidly fading. She
could only feel his strength, his completely male
domination. His mouth, with brutal cruelty, smothered
her moans of protest, forcing her lips to part as he
demanded total submission. She went ice-cold, then
red-hot, her head clouding, her ears singing as the
heated blood sped through her veins.

She heard his breath coming rough and thick as his
lips slid to her throat, as he bent her back over his arm.
'Scott—please . . .' she whispered, hardly knowing what
she was pleading for.

He lifted his head to look at her, his eyes glowing
hotly. 'Please what?' he asked tersely.

'You'll regret this,' she breathed incoherently,
despairing that this was all she could manage when she
really wanted to shout at him to let her go. Her mind
and her body were splitting down the middle. Her mind
was ordering her body to regain control, but her body
was taking no notice. It was laughing at her, telling her
she wanted Scott's kisses, more than anything she had
ever wanted in her life.

'I never waste time on regrets,' she heard Scott
drawling mockingly. 'Life's too short.'

Hotly he went on kissing her, her mouth, her face,
her neck. At the angle she was lying, her dark hair
spilled on to the cushion behind her and he ran his
fingers through it before his hands slid down to begin
exploring the outer curves of her breasts. Slowly he
moved inexorably inwards until he was brushing the
sensitive tips, where nerve ends leapt in response to his
touch. Sherry gasped as a white-hot desire flooded
through her and the pitiful remnants of her common
sense rapidly disappeared. She trembled as the sensual

tension between them became like an electric force, threatening to burn them up in the next second.

She couldn't speak, she was too dizzy with pleasure. Her arms went round his neck, her hands tangling in his thick black hair, her mind clouding with an urgency that made her bones melt.

Scott's arms tightened around her. He got up, carrying her, striding with her across the hall before she knew what he was doing, and a breath of sanity returned as she looked in alarm at the strong features above her.

'Where are you going?'

He stared at her. 'You must know the answer to that.'

He was going in the direction of the stairs and scorning her own stupidity, Sherry began wildly to struggle, her anxiety increasing as he wouldn't let her go. 'Scott,' she gasped, trembling, 'put me down!'

He paused at the foot of the stairs and began kissing her sensuously, his mouth making a mockery of her lingering protests. 'You want me. Whenever we're together I'm aware of it. You can't hide it from me, Sherry—I've had too much experience.'

'Don't, Scott,' she whispered, but as his hand slipped to her breast her breath caught in a betraying shiver of pleasure. Her half-closed eyes quickened his breathing while she clung to him in wordless capitulation.

Without another word he climbed the stairs, the silence of the house closing about them. Sherry lay in his arms, dizzy with an explosive mixture of fear and excitement. She wanted to fight him, the feeble voice of caution warned her to, but even though she knew she would be sorry later, at the moment her need seemed as great as his.

Scott walked straight into his bedroom and put her down on the bed. It was a huge bed and Sherry felt herself sinking into it. Her arms stiffened as he sank down beside her and began taking off her blouse, but she didn't attempt to evade his swiftly moving hands. Soon she was naked, her clothes a small heap on the floor, but she could only gaze at him numbly.

He sat quite still, his glance leaping over her, taking in her smooth-skinned beauty, the narrow curves of her waist and hips, the gentle swell of her breasts. She heard his harsh intake of breath and her eyes closed weakly as her body burned briefly in shock. She was aching for him to make love to her, but she didn't try and pretend it wouldn't be a step into the unknown. She was afraid, but her desire for him was so strong she couldn't even beg him to be gentle with her.

She lay naked and unmoving as his hands went impatiently to his own clothing, stripping it off and tossing it aside. Her eyes clung in revealing fascination to his hard, tanned body until an awareness of what she was doing brought a swift flush to her cheeks and she turned quickly over.

She felt his weight come nearer as he lay down by her side and turned her back to him. He put his arms round her, pulling her against him again, kissing her deeply before pushing her back on the pillows. From her lips, his mouth traced an insistent path to her breasts, and a piercing sensation went through her as he caressed them gently. One hand began stroking the warm skin of her inner thigh, seductively coaxing, while his other tugged her head back as he crushed her mouth open to his searching, demanding kisses. She could feel the passion and desire in him as he groaned and his arms held her fiercely.

Equally fiercely Sherry responded, her fingernails digging into the powerful muscles of his back. Reality was falling away from her, as was all restraint. She could hear small noises escaping her throat as her hands pressed him down upon her so that she was crushed against the hurting hardness of his entire length. His lips blazed a trail of passion across her cheek as he pushed his face into the fragrant silk of her hair.

'How often have you done this before, Sherry?'

Somehow, she could never afterwards say why, his savage question shocked her incredibly. 'I haven't,' she choked, feeling herself go rigid.

'Sherry!' He rolled off her slightly, suddenly a determined glint in the darkness of his eyes. 'I don't want any more lies.'

Sherry stared at him, her nerves jumping sickeningly as she realised he didn't believe her. She shivered as a chill swept over her and hastily she began to pull herself together. She could see how she had been about to make a terrible mistake. How could she, even for a moment, having been tempted to give herself to a man who didn't love her?

'I don't tell lies,' she retorted unevenly. 'But you don't have to believe me.'

'I bloody well don't!' he said harshly. 'At least you aren't pretending to love me.'

'I hate you!' she whispered, so wounded by his savage attack that she actually felt she did. She stared at him, her blue eyes dilated in anguish and horror.

'Don't look at me like that,' Scott rapped out, his arms reaching for her again. 'Hell, does it matter whether we hate each other or not? Emotions are for those with more serious commitments in mind.'

Evading his impatient arms, Sherry leapt out of bed, automatically sweeping up her clothes as she ran to the door. Remembering where the bathroom was, from the times she had been here before, she fled into it and locked the door. Pulling on her blouse and skirt with hands that shook, she threw back her hair and rushed out again.

Scott was waiting outside—she nearly collided with him. He had been even quicker in getting dressed than she had. She had hoped he might have had the decency to stay out of sight until she had gone, but he wasn't a man, she thought bitterly, to be deprived of the last word!

After one startled glance at him, she turned in the direction of the stairs, but he caught her arm.

'Not so fast, Sherry,' he said tersely. 'Are you quite sure you want to go?'

'Quite sure,' she replied woodenly, realising with a start of amazement that he might be asking her to stay.

'Very well,' his face hardened and he was suddenly a stranger. 'I won't detain you.'

'I'm sorry,' she whispered, unable to tear her eyes from him, yet angry with herself for hesitating. 'I'm sorry,' she repeated helplessly.

Scott's mouth tightened. 'Don't be,' he mocked. 'There's never any shortage of women—willing ones, I mean.'

Sherry didn't remember how she got out of the house, into the truck and home to Googon. She supposed it must have been because the roads were empty that she managed the journey safely, for half the time she couldn't see for tears. They ran down her cheeks and kept on flowing, springing rawly from a bleeding wound inside her. She tried to pull herself together, but to no avail. She ought to be thankful, shouldn't she, that she hadn't succumbed to Scott's demands? He had tried to force himself on her and she'd been lucky to escape!

No, that wasn't quite true, she admitted painfully. Scott had wanted her, but she could have put up a greater fight. She had angered him, but she was sure he hadn't meant to do more than kiss her; she couldn't understand how everything had got so out of hand. Her own response must have had something to do with it, and under his iron control, Scott was a very virile man. It was no use blaming him entirely for what had happened.

Perhaps she should be grateful instead of condemning him completely. If his accusations hadn't jerked her rudely from the euphoric daze she'd been in, she might have belonged to him now, and his harsh opinion of her could only have turned his lovemaking into an act of contempt. Hadn't he made it quite clear, as well, that for him there was no commitment? She could never have said she hadn't been warned! If she had given herself to him, he would have considered her an hour's entertainment, nothing more!

She pulled her hat well down over her eyes next morning, as she went to help Sam. The men were all so busy she didn't really think they would have time to notice she had cried all night, but she tried to avoid any possible speculation. Seemingly no one guessed she had been to Coomarlee until after midnight, and she didn't mention it to anyone.

After lunch Sam said some supplies were urgently needed, so she went to get them from Bourke. The town was busy and she spotted several people she knew, though she tried to avoid them. She still felt too shaken from the night before to be sociable. It was when she had darted down a shadowy cutting to escape a particularly garrulous acquaintance that she saw Scott strolling past, a radiant Dulcie Easten clinging tightly to his arm.

That was all she needed! Sherry thought, enraged, trying to build herself up into a fury rather than burst into tears again. Scott certainly hadn't been long in seeking more rewarding company. She wondered how she would have felt if she had spent the night in his arms and then bumped into him, no doubt easing a guilty conscience with the woman he was considering marrying.

Unfortunately, because she was so stricken by what she had seen, she wasn't able to evade the next person who bore down on her.

Mary Armstrong exclaimed. 'Just the very person I wanted to see! I rang you but couldn't get an answer. You must have been out.'

'We've been busy with the shearing,' Sherry tried to smile as if she hadn't a care in the world. 'How are you?'

The other girl grimaced. 'Packing, getting ready for our European trip like mad. I'm completely exhausted, my dear!' She laughed gaily, belying this, her brown eyes warm and friendly. 'In the midst of all my wild preparations, which Simon tells me every time he sees me is crazy, we want to have a bit of a farewell do. Just a buffet, you know, and a bit of dancing, nothing elaborate, and I've been trying to get hold of you to see if you can come.'

Sherry saw she wasn't going to get out of it, and she did think for a moment that a party might cheer her up, until she realised Scott was sure to be there.

'It's going to be difficult,' she hedged uneasily. 'It's a long way.'

'That's no problem,' Mary grinned. 'I'd already thought of it. I'll ask Bill Danvers from Dalton Downs to pick you up—he's coming with his wife. I was going to beg you a lift from Scott Brady, but I've just seen him and he's bringing Dulcie Easten. We're all waiting breathlessly for the announcement of their engagement, so I daren't ask him to collect you. He'd hardly take kindly to popping the question with you sitting beside them!'

Laughing, she went on her way, not noticing how pale Sherry had gone. So Scott was going to marry Dulcie, after all? Well, she had known it was going to happen so she couldn't pretend to be surprised; she only wished it didn't hurt as much. It would be even worse if Scott brought Dulcie to live at Coomarlee, but at least there would be some distance between them. It wasn't like living next door in England.

In a mood of brooding defiance, she went and bought herself a silky skirt and top. Suddenly she was determined no one should think she was too poor to afford a new dress. She didn't go mad; she got something very modestly priced, but even so it was nice. Nick Wallace was going to have a fit, but she wasn't going to worry about that immediately. With luck, if she didn't do it again, he might not notice that the cheque was made out for clothes and not necessities.

She worked so hard the following day, in an attempt to forget Scott and what had happened at Coomarlee, that by evening she was exhausted. She felt so tired she almost rang the Danvers and told them not to call for her. It took a lot of willpower to force herself to take a shower instead. The shower did make her feel better, and, refusing to be a coward, she resolutely got into her new outfit.

With a sense of awe, she realised she looked quite elegant. The skirt and top clung to the slender lines of her figure as though they'd been specially made for her. She was too thin and pale, of course, but with her hair brushed to a shining cloud and her eyes and mouth lightly made up, her paleness wasn't so noticeable. It was courage she was really lacking. The thought of meeting Scott again nearly drove her to sample what was left of Kim's whisky, but as she waited for the Danvers to arrive, she settled for a cup of black coffee. Any boost she might get from something stronger would have worn off before she reached the party, and perhaps a level head and a little pride might do more for her.

The Danvers had their own plane and picked Sherry up at exactly the time they had arranged. They were a nice couple and seemed to take to her at once. She was invited to a party they were giving, in a few weeks' time, before they even reached Mary and Simon's station. Their friendliness made Sherry aware that it might have been chiefly her grandfather's anti-social inclinations that had been responsible for her getting so few invitations in the past.

The party was already in full swing when they arrived and Mary and Simon were there to meet them. Otherwise, as Mary had warned, it was a very casual affair. A large buffet was spread on tables in the dining-room, nothing elaborate but appetising, and in sufficient quantities to feed an army. In another large room, people were dancing, spilling outside on the wide verandas and terraces that led to the garden. The house, on the whole, wasn't huge or luxuriously furnished, but Sherry liked it on sight, for it was so homely, giving an immediate impression of warmth. The Armstrongs didn't appear to have a housekeeper, just a couple of maids with Mary supervising herself.

Some of the guests Sherry had met before, at Coomarlee, but on the whole, the average age of those here tonight was much younger. A lot of them were in their early twenties and laughed and talked a lot, obviously bent on enjoying themselves. Dulcie, when she walked in with Scott, made a beeline for the more sedate faction, dragging Scott with her. Sherry, who happened to be looking their way at the time, swallowed and turned her back, telling herself, as always, that it would have been a lot worse if she had let Scott make love to her.

She danced with several young men who couldn't think where she had been all their lives. To her surprise she found herself popular. She was asked for dates so many times she began to lose count. After years of comparative isolation, it took a lot of getting used to.

After a little while she went to ask Mary if she could help with anything.

'Thanks, but no, love,' Mary smiled gratefully. 'Surprisingly, you're the first one who's offered. The food's all ready to serve in an hour. You can give a hand with the coffee then, if you like.'

Sherry said she'd be pleased to and Mary glanced at her, suddenly scrutinising her closely. 'I must say you appear to be the belle of the ball! I never realised we'd a proper English beauty in our midst.'

Mary was only teasing, Sherry knew, so she managed a faint smile. 'I'm only half English, you know. And since coming to live at Googon, I consider myself wholly Australian. Although Scott,' she added, with a touch of unconscious bitterness, 'doesn't think so.'

'Doesn't he?' Mary's expressive brows rose. 'Don't you get on, you two?' she queried, in seeming innocence.

Sherry bit her lip. 'Not really. Scott doesn't like me.'

'So that's what it is!' Mary seemed to pounce on something that had been puzzling her. 'I was wondering why he was keeping you under constant surveillance. Is he watching to see you don't corrupt our susceptible young males?'

Sherry laughed hollowly. 'I think you're having me on!'

Mary grinned. 'Oh, by the way,' she murmured, lowering her voice with a quick glance over her shoulder to make sure she couldn't be overheard, 'what's all this about Scott's sister? We read the announcement of her marriage in the papers, but Scott's keeping awfully quiet about it and I haven't the courage to ask him outright. Someone told me, weeks ago, that Ellen was friendly with your brother, then we heard he'd disappeared.'

Wondering how she was supposed to reply to that, Sherry tried to stay composed. 'They were friendly,' she said, 'but Kim's gone to England. He might be away for a while.'

'Whew!' Mary stared at her. 'How on earth are you going to manage on your own?'

It was a question Sherry knew she was going to hear frequently. 'I've got a good man. He managed for my grandfather before he died, and I know I can rely on him.'

Mary didn't attempt to dispute it, or ask anything more about Ellen. Much to Sherry's relief, she seemed more diverted by Sherry being alone on Googon. 'If you ever need any help or advice,' she said kindly, her eyes warm with concern, 'you're welcome to give us a ring. It's sometimes good just to have someone to talk

to. I know what I felt like after my parents died, before
I met Simon.'

'You have Simon now, though.'

'Umm,' Mary laughed, 'he's my safety valve. I pour
out my troubles in his willing—or unwilling—ears. I
don't know what I'd do without him. If ever I lost
him . . .'

'Hi,' Sherry interrupted humorously, 'you're going on
a trip, remember!'

'So I am,' Mary laughed wryly. 'I guess I'm just too
excited.'

'I expect Simon is too.'

'Yes,' Mary nodded, but she also frowned. 'He's a bit
worried about this excessive heat, though. It's worse
farther south, I believe.'

Sherry recalled Scott mentioning the risk of fire after
he'd been to Melbourne. He had glossed over it quickly,
but she thought now that that might have been because
she'd looked anxious rather than that there was no real
threat. She felt anxious again, but some late arrivals
claimed Mary's attention before they could talk about
it.

As the party rapidly got into full swing, Sherry talked
and laughed, but all the time her eyes were drawn like a
magnet to Scott. Dulcie didn't leave his side, but they
weren't dancing. The group they were in were probably
discussing everything under the sun, which wasn't in
itself surprising, for Australians, on the whole, enjoyed
nothing better than talking and arguing, but it did
surprise Sherry that Scott was missing so many
opportunities to have Dulcie in his arms.

Watching him, Sherry felt her heart contract. He was
tall, dark and cruelly handsome, with the cool
assurance that comes from complete self-confidence. He
was a man everyone looked up to, a born leader, who
accepted his place in the world, along with its ensuing
responsibilities which would make many other men
shrink. Whoever Scott Brady married would have to be

able to live up to him. Instinctively Sherry knew she could do this, especially with a little practice, but he only wanted an affair with her, he didn't want her for his wife. As he sensed her unhappy observation, his glance swung in her direction, but there was nothing in his expression, one way or another, apart from perhaps condemnation. Sherry winced as a piercing shaft of it went right through her.

Believing he would never speak to her again unless it was absolutely necessary, she was startled to find him beside her as she was helping herself half-heartedly to various dishes at supper. She went so weak, she had no strength to stop him when he removed her plate from her hands and began filling it up.

'You're too thin,' he said firmly. 'You have to eat properly.'

She flushed, aware of Dulcie hovering glacially, and stared in consternation at her plate. 'I can't eat all this!'

'You can try,' Scott retorted, unrelentingly.

Helplessly Sherry shrugged as her eyes rose to meet his. Her heart leapt sickeningly in her breast, but his expression didn't alter. She straightened and set about eating her meal, forcing herself to swallow each mouthful. She tried to keep her mind blank, hoping he would have the decency to leave her, but he stayed by her side. The silence might have been of concrete, the effort it took to break it. 'It—it's a nice party.'

He merely lifted his dark brows slightly, his lips thinning.

Dulcie tugged at his arm, pouting. 'Could you get me something as well, darling? Mind you,' her lashes half fell over her eyes, hiding a malicious glitter, 'I don't eat nearly as much as Miss Grant. My appetite's not as huge as all that.'

'Of course,' Scott complied smoothly, his eyes still on Sherry. 'Your appetite would never match hers.'

Sherry felt her cheeks grow scarlet and her anger could scarcely be contained. How could he remind her so blatantly of her own sensuousness! Especially when he was responsible for making her aware of it. She didn't retaliate but made no attempt to hide that she considered him an insensitive brute!

He even had the nerve to call frostily, as she walked away in order to give him room to serve Dulcie, 'Save a dance for me later, Sherry.'

Not if I can help it, Sherry thought, pretending not to hear, and doing her best, afterwards, to give the impression she was enjoying herself madly, so that he would discard any idea of coming after her.

He did come, though, and not one of her eager young partners was willing to oppose him as he swept her from them, his arms tightening possessively round her. She stiffened with resentment at the ruthlessness with which he parted her from people who had only been trying to give her a good time.

He looked down on her broodingly, not a trace of humour in his eyes. He studied her new image, her silky skirt and matching top, its low cleavage exposing the shadowed cleft between her pale breasts. Then his glance rose higher to take in her air of nervous delicacy, the extreme beauty of her face. 'I like your—dress,' he said softly, his eyes on her breasts again. 'Is it new?'

'How did you guess?' she asked acidly, knowing her heart was accelerating visibly and furious that she couldn't control it.

'You could do with a whole new wardrobe.' He still spoke softly but his eyes narrowed. 'Would you let me supply it?'

'No, thank you,' she managed coolly, thinking how wrong she had been. She had thought she wouldn't see him again, but it seemed he didn't give up easily. Well, if he thought he could buy her, he could think again!

'You were always pretty,' he mused, as if he hadn't heard her, 'but tonight you're beautiful. With a little more grooming, jewellery and the right clothes, you'd be all any man could want. Even without,' he observed

mockingly, 'no man in his right senses would ever look
at anyone else.'

He must be the devil incarnate, that even a few such
words from him should make her feel weak. For the
second time that evening he had succeeded in depriving
her of strength. 'I'm not interested in being someone's
mistress,' she retaliated, the colour in her cheeks flaring
afresh.

His mouth quirked, but what with, it was difficult to
tell. He made no comment on her terse little statement,
but just when she began hoping he would simply dance
with her and let her go, he attacked sardonically from
another direction.

'You appear to be enjoying yourself this evening.'

Biting her lip on a cutting retort, Sherry restrained
herself to murmuring tightly, 'Any reason why I
shouldn't?'

He gave her a hard stare. 'Are you looking for
someone to provide the help you rejected from me?'

The taunt made her flush angrily. 'That's not fair!' she
said fiercely. 'I still have the cook you sent and I didn't
refuse your help in buying a truck.'

Curtly he retorted, 'I didn't fall down on my side of
the bargain. If I asked for repayment it wasn't in kind,
but even so, you declined to give it.'

'Was it repayment you were asking—at Coomarlee?'
she asked, equally coldly.

'Ah,' Scott smiled savagely, 'I wondered when you'd
get round to that.'

'What did you expect?' she asked bitterly, her voice
rising.'

'Shut up,' he muttered, beginning to dance with her
in earnest, sweeping her along with the cool mastery she
found so attractive yet irritating. 'You're attracting
attention. We don't have to fight here.'

He pulled her closer and Sherry fought him, but only
for a few seconds. Her body burned with resentment,
but she surrendered to an irresistible desire to be close

to him again. Every time she saw him might be the last. Now, as his hand moved across the silken skin of her back, a feeling of desperation replaced that of anger, making her surrender weakly as his cheek touched her hair. The powerful arms holding her tightened and she felt him moving in on her as he heard her indrawn breath.

They looked at each other once and kept on dancing. Sherry was hardly aware of anyone else in the room. Her eyes closed, her body following the movements of his as if they were one, and her pulses leapt whenever Scott's mouth feathered her cheek. She couldn't think, she could only feel, and she didn't care what she was betraying. Aching with love for him as she was, it didn't seem to matter whether he cared one iota for her or not. She was only aware of her body melting sensuously and of the answering emotion she could feel in him.

When the music stopped, still without speaking, Scott guided her out along the terrace, not far from the house but far enough to escape curious eyes. When she realised the direction he was taking her, she held back, not wanting to go anywhere with him.

On a curt breath, he muttered, 'Behave yourself, Sherry. Are you bent on attracting attention? If you must quarrel with me, wait till we get out of sight.'

'Have you ever thought Miss Easten might be planning my demise?' she choked, as darkness enclosed them.

'Why should she?' he asked arrogantly, steering her under the shadowy, concealing branches of an obliging tree.

'You brought her, didn't you?' Sherry pointed out tersely. 'It would seem you enjoy having us all on . . .'

'Yes?' His eyes gleamed with anger as she hesitated. 'What is it I enjoy with such diabolical pleasure as you imply?'

'Having us all on a string!' she cried recklessly.

'For all the good it does me!' he retorted

enigmatically, staring at her in the dim light. 'And, for your information, I was asked to bring Dulcie along, and, as she trotted up just as I was about to refuse, I found myself in what's commonly known as a bit of a quandary.'

'I didn't think you were a man frightened to speak his mind,' Sherry said mutinously. She could see Dulcie gliding along, insinuating herself with all the guile of a beautiful, poisonous snake, but she couldn't forgive him for capitulating.

'Over anything I consider important, I generally do,' he said repressively. 'If it hadn't been that Simon Armstrong is a friend, I shouldn't have been here this evening, but as I was coming it would have been rather churlish to refuse anyone a lift.'

'Especially the girl you're hoping to marry!' Sherry felt driven to let him know he wasn't fooling her. For some reason it was suiting him to pretend Dulcie meant nothing to him, but she knew better. It made her feel sick, but then, she supposed, sickness was all a part of unrequited love. That had such an old-fashioned ring to it that a wave of mirthless laughter went through her, to be stilled as Scott said curtly,

'I don't intend marrying Dulcie Easten.'

Sherry's throat clogged in surprise. 'You—don't?'

'No.'

'But,' she trembled as his steely fingers bit into her arm, 'you gave the impression . . .'

He interrupted cynically, 'Haven't we had this conversation before? Have I ever said anything definite about marrying anybody? People, yourself apparently included, frequently jump to the wrong conclusions, which I've neither the time or inclination to deny. Most personable males have this kind of thing to endure and I don't let it bother me, but it seems to be bothering you.'

Sherry didn't care about rumours, but she found

what Scott was telling her incredible. Her heart leapt with relief and gladness, for a moment allowed to be rampant. Then her brief glow of happiness faded. That Scott wasn't marrying Dulcie Easten didn't mean he had someone else in mind.

'Maybe one day you'll meet the right girl,' she whispered bleakly, 'and marry her.'

'When I meet someone who cares for me enough,' he replied, his eyes piercing the darkness to her taut face.

She glanced up, blue eyes widening. 'What would you consider enough?'

'You mean how would I measure the depth of her feelings?'

Nodding miserably, Sherry clenched her hands. She felt he was getting at her, choosing his words deliberately to mock her, knowing how she felt about him.

'I'd like her to be willing to sacrifice everything,' the cool, taunting voice went on, 'without making stipulations, or holding anything back.'

'You're asking a lot,' she whispered hollowly, in no doubt as to what he was hinting at.

Cruelly he caught her to him, his hands insistent on her waist, his breath on her face. She could feel a certain puzzling tension in him, despite his crisp rejoiner. 'She would be amply rewarded.'

Her eyes fell in front of his fixed stare as she tried to pull herself together, trembling. 'I can't believe a man like you would ask someone to prove their love, like the hero of a second-rate novel.'

'You're getting everything out of context,' he snapped. 'All I'm asking for is mutual trust.'

'And afterwards you would laugh and conveniently forget any promises you made,' Sherry said coldly.

CHAPTER TEN

THEY stood staring at each other like enemies, under the sweeping branches of the tree. Then, with a muttered curse, Scott's mouth found hers and she was drawn tightly against his hard, lean body. His lips were hard and cool, taking everything but giving nothing. He ravaged her mouth, his arms pressing her possessively closer, his palms flat on the heated flesh of her back as passion flamed and leapt between them.

Sherry thought he murmured something that sounded like, 'I've got to have you,' but she couldn't be sure. Her pulses were beating so loudly she couldn't clearly hear anything else. A hungry urgency invaded her, increasing in depth until she panicked, becoming afraid. She began pulling away, trying desperately to free herself.

He let her fight until all her strength had gone and she lay spent against him, catching her breath in great sobbing gasps of fear and shame.

'Do you still deny you want me?' he asked thickly.

'No,' she gulped distractedly, 'but I won't have an affair with you.'

'You believe I'd ask you to?'

'Yes.'

'Then you don't even know me,' he said harshly. 'And until your opinion of me changes, we might be better apart.' He kissed her mouth once more, forcing it open beneath his before pushing her away, wiping his lips with the back of his hand. 'Run along,' he said derisively, 'and concentrate on growing up. Until then you won't be much use to anyone.'

Sherry was startled the following afternoon—if any

emotion could penetrate the raw state of numbness she was in—when Dulcie turned up at Googon. When Leda came to tell her she had a visitor, she had to ask twice before she could feel convinced it really was Miss Easten visiting their humble abode.

'Where is she now?' she asked quickly, following the little Aborigine girl from the shearing sheds.

'I put her in the living-room,' Leda grinned, 'but she doesn't look too happy, Miss Sherry.'

Dulcie didn't. She was sitting on the edge of a chair looking about her disdainfully. Sherry wondered what could have brought her here just a few hours after a party that had gone on until almost dawn, when normally, Sherry suspected, Dulcie would have still been in bed.

She hadn't long to wait to find out.

'I saw you drop this, last night,' Dulcie quite blatantly drew from her bag a handkerchief Sherry had never seen before. 'It's exquisite, isn't it?' She gave the impression of being quite overcome by admiration as she held out the lace-edged square. 'I was passing and I guessed how miserable you must be, believing you'd lost it.'

For a moment Sherry gazed at it, frowning, then she said quietly, 'I'm afraid you've had a wasted journey. It isn't mine.'

Dulcie put on a charming little act of consternation while Sherry waited patiently to hear the true purpose of her visit. Leda brought coffee, and she poured it carefully, hoping Dulcie would soon get to the point and leave. Then ashamed of such inhospitable thoughts towards someone who hadn't really done her any harm, she forced a warmer note in her voice.

'It was good of you to go to so much trouble, anyway.'

They both knew the handkerchief was an excuse, and Sherry was relieved when, after tucking it back in her bag and accepting the cup of coffee Sherry passed her,

Dulcie said, more truthfully this time, 'I really came to speak to you about Scott.'

'I see,' Sherry said noncommittally. She didn't want to even think about Scott, after last night, but she could see Dulcie had something on her mind and wasn't going to be satisfied until she had at least given it an airing.

'Scott's always been fond of me,' Dulcie began coolly.

'Yes,' Sherry murmured.

'Lately, though,' Dulcie continued pensively, 'he's been different.'

'How—different?' Sherry asked cautiously.

Dulcie's lips set sulkily. 'He's been neglecting me the tiniest little bit, and I don't like it.'

Sherry sighed, wondering exactly what Dulcie was up to. 'I'm not sure why you're telling me this, Miss Easten.'

'He needs a wife, you know,' Dulcie said suddenly. 'His first wife put him off marriage, but I think he'll get round to trying again—with me, if you don't interfere.'

It was a hot day, but Sherry felt herself go cold. Dulcie, had she but known it, had nothing to fear from her. 'How could anything I do make any difference?' she asked tonelessly.

For once Dulcie seemed ill at ease, then she frowned more belligerently. 'Well, you often appear to be in need of assistance. You take up a lot of his time and I have a feeling, that for some reason or another, he imagines he's responsible for what happens to you. I think,' she concluded impatiently, 'it has something to do with this mysterious business of his sister and your brother.'

Sherry wasn't going into that! 'I'm sure you're mistaken,' she retorted coldly. 'Since Kim went back to England, Scott has helped me a few times, but he does the same for other people. I think you'll find that from now on I'll be able to manage without further assistance.'

'Oh, good!' Dulcie immediately looked happier. 'I'm glad to hear it.' She glanced quickly at her watch, revealing that she was thinking of leaving. 'Did you know that Scott's off to a conference in Melbourne today? He told me last night, and I'm wondering if he was hinting that I should join him.'

Suddenly Sherry felt sorry for the other girl as well as herself. Scott had dallied with them both without having any serious intentions, but if Dulcie wasn't aware of that then it certainly wasn't her place to tell her. Underneath Dulcie's hard sophistication, she wasn't sure of Scott at all, which must be why she was here today, groping blindly for the kind of assurance only he could give. Sherry didn't think Scott had been lying, in the Armstrongs' garden, when he had said emphatically that he wouldn't be marrying Dulcie, but it might be kinder to let her continue living in a fool's paradise, as long as she was able.

When Dulcie had gone, Sherry returned to the work she had abandoned to talk to her. She didn't feel happy, but she did have an increasing sense of righteousness to comfort her. Dulcie had hinted, before she left, at having slept with Scott, and Sherry guessed she wouldn't be the only one to have succumbed to his blatant charm. If she had given in to him, she would have become just another in a long line of women who imagined they had an important place in his life but whom he discarded with eventual contempt.

It amazed Sherry that after a week, with such a record of his callousness continually before her, she missed him so much that she almost craved for the sight of him. Trying to counteract this with hard work made her grow so thin that even Sam began looking at her in alarm. To alleviate his anxiety, which she realised he might be too embarrassed to put in words, she took to using a little blusher on her cheeks and tried to eat more. Sometimes she wished the Armstrongs hadn't been away. There were times when she would have given anything to have been able to talk to Mary, even about something as predictable as the Australian weather.

She nearly dropped when, one morning, Mary rang her. Thinking, incredibly, that she must be ringing from London, she was surprised again when Mary told her she was still at home.

'We haven't gone,' she confessed. 'At the last moment Simon balked. He couldn't get rid of the feeling that there might be a fire. He was extremely worried, not only because of our place, and he said if there was an outbreak anywhere in the state he would feel like a rat deserting a sinking ship. I'll admit I was disappointed, but I've too healthy a respect for Simon's intuition to disregard it altogether. And you'll have seen, this morning, he's been proved right. That's why I'm ringing.'

Sherry drew a sharp breath, overwhelmed by a nameless dread, worse than the usual reaction to the news of fire. She clutched the receiver tightly. 'I hadn't heard anything, I've been out since before six. Whereabouts have the fires started?'

'Farther south, nearer Melbourne.'

'Melbourne?' Now Sherry understood her terrible feeling of dread. 'Scott's down there!'

'Yes,' Mary said grimly. 'Simon's been trying to get hold of him, but the lines are so busy he hasn't been able to get through.'

'Will he be able to later——'

'Perhaps——' Mary hesitated, as if sensing Sherry's extreme anxiety. 'The thing is, if the fires aren't controlled, the lines will become blocked with people enquiring about relations and friends, and we might have to wait, which isn't easy. Simon's talking of going to Melbourne himself.'

'I wish I could,' Sherry said helplessly.

'You're better where you are,' Mary retorted almost sharply. 'And try not to worry too much. Would you like to come and stay with us?'

'Oh, no,' Sherry exclaimed. 'I mean, it's kind of you, but I couldn't leave Googon. I'd be grateful, though, if you'd give me a ring as soon as you have news of Scott.'

If Mary thought it an odd request, she didn't say so, and Sherry suspected Mary had known all along that she loved him.

The period after that was one of the worst Sherry had ever lived through. All Simon discovered was that Scott, along with hundreds of others, was helping to fight the terrible fires which were spreading rapidly, causing terrifying devastation. Mary kept in constant touch. Simon, she said, was working night and day, organising fire patrols in the district and assisting wherever he could. They heard horrific stories of men fighting until they were exhausted against the racing, uncontrollable flames and returning home to find their families lost, together with their property and stock. There were so many incidents of heroism, self-sacrifice and endurance that no one could fail to be moved by it. Sherry felt the whole nation must be weeping, yet at the same time incredibly proud.

Eventually the degree of worry she experienced over the fires and Scott became so extreme that when news came that he had been injured, she almost passed out.

The first she knew of it was when Mary and Simon flew to Googon to see her. They were in the living-room when she suddenly realised they had something to tell her. 'It's about Scott,' Mary said gently, when she asked anxiously what it was.

'Where is he?' Sherry trembled, going quite white.

'The thing is, we don't know,' Mary replied tautly. 'We only heard he was with a rescue team and got hurt.'

'Oh, no!' The room whirled and Sherry reeled. From a great distance she heard Mary saying urgently, 'Is there any brandy, do you think?'

Sherry fought her way back through the darkness

enclosing her, trying to get a grip on herself. 'I'm all right,' she said faintly.

Simon returned with some brandy which Mary insisted she swallowed. Then she sent Simon off again to make some tea. 'Good and strong!' she called after him.

The brandy helped, but Sherry wished she hadn't fainted as she must have given too much away. She bit her lip hard to stop crying as she thought of the pain Scott might be in, but she failed to hide her distress from Mary.

Mary, as Sherry had suspected, knew more about her feelings for Scott than she had revealed. 'Stop worrying, Sherry,' she said with gentle asperity. 'You don't have to pretend to be brave with me. I guessed a long time ago that you're in love with him.'

After they had gone, Sherry went through another little hell with her conscience. Scott might have died, he must still be in danger. He had risked his life, been prepared to give it that others might live. He might just be one of those who had shown extreme courage and disregard for their own safety, in the present crisis, but it didn't make her feel any better that he had been prepared to give so much while she had been willing to give so little. When he had needed her, she had only thought of herself, and now she must be prepared to live with the knowledge of her own selfishness. The hours, maybe days, of waiting before it was discovered whether he was alive or dead, might be just punishment.

It was another twenty-four hours before Simon managed to discover where Scott was and learnt something of his condition. He had had an amazing escape, though he was suffering from concussion and burns and might be in hospital for a while.

Sherry would have given all she possessed to have been able to visit him. When Simon rang she almost wept. 'There must be some possibility of seeing him!' she cried desperately, but Simon was adamant. Scott, he said, absolutely forbade it.

If Scott hadn't arrived home at the end of the week, Sherry had been going to disregard such orders and go to Melbourne to see him, no matter how difficult it might prove to be. She was actually getting ready when Mary rang and said he was back.

'At—Coomarlee?' whispered Sherry, her throat so tight she could hardly speak.

'At Coomarlee,' Mary assured her gently.

The truck couldn't go fast enough. It was late evening and she had showered and put on a light robe before starting to get together a few things for the journey she had intended making in the morning. It was only necessary to put on a pair of clean jeans and she was ready.

Darkness was falling as she reached Coomarlee. Mrs Fox answered the door herself, a much kinder light in her eyes than Sherry had ever seen, as she quietly asked Sherry to come in.

'Scott . . .?' Sherry spoke his name, discovering painfully that it was all she could manage.

'Don't worry,' Mrs Fox spoke with unexpected gentleness, 'we've all been anxious, but he was hoping you would call. I'm just off to my own quarters, but he said, if you did come, to send you straight up.' As Sherry swayed, she added with concern, 'Can I make you some coffee or get you a drink?'

Numbly Sherry shook her head. 'Oh, no. No, thank you.'

'It's the door at the far end of the corridor,' Mrs Fox smiled. 'He's almost recovered—just a bit tired, I think.'

Sherry scarcely heard as she ran up the stairs. In the distance a door opened and closed, beyond the kitchen, as Mrs Fox left, but Sherry never paused.

Finding Scott's room, she thought vaguely that Mrs Fox wouldn't know she had been here before. She was hurrying straight in when she hesitated, flushed with doubt. Despite Mrs Fox's assurance, Scott might not be pleased to see her at this hour. He might not like it, anyway, if she barged straight in.

It was about her last coherent thought. Taking a deep breath, she knocked and received an order to enter. When she did and found him sitting in his bathrobe, reading some mail, she swayed dizzily.

'Sherry!' As she stood staring helplessly, he sprang to his feet, scattering letters carelessly on the floor. His face swam above her, pale, but as forceful as ever, then she was in his arms.

For a long moment they didn't speak, just held on to each other, as if just being near each other was enough. But instead of dissipating the desperate feeling between them, proximity increased it. Scott had been ill, but she forgot as the savage cruelty of his embrace crushed her with a fervour that mounted to a kind of mindless ferocity.

It was as if their bodies craved each other and had been too long apart. There was no room for tenderness and Sherry didn't even think of it. Scott's hand touched her throat, lifting her chin, his mouth finding hers with a driving force that made her whimper. She trembled at his burning need for satisfaction and felt him shaking against her.

'Do you love me?' he whispered hoarsely, and she groaned, 'Yes, I do,' knowing, whatever else happened, she could no longer deny the truth.

A moment later she was flung across the bed, his body following hers as they kissed urgently, both full of explosive desire. Sherry's one wish was to belong to him, and unconsciously she did everything to prove it. She wound her arms round his neck, clinging to him convulsively, mouth open, shuddering.

Scott began pulling off their clothes, hers first, then his. Within minutes their bodies were glazed with heat, their skin moist with perspiration. Sherry heard the harsh intake of his breath as his head burrowed between her breasts and she twisted restlessly, pressing herself closer. She was like a flame in his arms, her heart beating wildly under the heavier thunder of his. She heard him mutter something as his hands slid intimately over her and she felt her whole body leaping in hungry response.

His fingers circled her navel, then swept down her stomach, teasing unbearably. Giddily, when the sensation he was arousing grew too much to bear, she tried to break free of the sensuous web he was spinning so skilfully around her, but she was already trapped by the wild desire brought on by his touch. His other hand slid under her hips and she heard him groan as she melted against him, then coherent thought fled as he moved in ruthlessly to possess her.

She was helpless against his invasion and, for a brief moment, stunned by the pain of it, but as his mouth found hers again, her lips became soft and responsive as she was consumed by the demands of his powerful male body. Fiercely her hands gripped his bare brown shoulders and it was as though she had been taken over by some creature alien to herself. Feeling her surrender, Scott swept her along on an irresistible rush of sensation. She cried out as their bodies finally exploded in a volume of rapture so intense that she was rendered almost mindless by the force of it.

She must have fallen from a state of extreme reaction to a kind of drugged sleep, for when she woke, until she saw Scott lying beside her, she had no clear idea where she was. She remembered then how, after he had made love to her, he had started saying something but had seemed overwhelmed by a strange exhaustion. They must both have fallen asleep and slept soundly, although she didn't know for how long. For a moment she watched him, gazing intently at his beloved face. He looked tired but more relaxed than she had seen him, the lines about his eyes and mouth much erased.

She felt slow tears sting her eyes as she thought of the danger he had been in. A pang of remorse shook her that she hadn't even asked him how he was. Half dazed as she was with a complexity of emotions, it seemed she had again let him down. Mrs Fox had said he had hoped she would call, but instead of behaving in a proper manner and remembering how ill he had been—perhaps still was, she had rushed in here, thrown herself at him, and now, because of what had happened, he might easily have a relapse.

It appeared to Sherry that there wasn't a situation she could cope with at all well. She had assumed Scott would still want her, but now she would never know for sure. He had asked if she loved him and accepted her assurances that she did without giving any indication of his own feelings. He had been fighting fires and, apart from the injuries he had sustained, must be suffering from a certain amount of exhaustion and shock. Making love to someone had probably offered a kind of release which, in his weakened state, he had found impossible to resist.

Her cheeks hot, Sherry's head drooped. She had given in to him, met him more than halfway, even urged him on. Where were her high romantic principles now? She had offered herself to him shamefully, with a complete disregard of the consequences. She must have asked for all she got, and suddenly she couldn't bear to stay and witness his embarrassment when he woke up.

Stealthily she crept from his bed, refusing to allow herself to think any more of the ecstasy she had experienced there. She didn't take her clothes to the bathroom this time to put on, but dressed where she stood, trying, despite the clumsiness of her fingers, not to make a sound. She dared not kiss him, but forced herself to be content with a last yearning glance before hurrying from the house.

Outside it was dark and she paused briefly, lifting her taut face to a drift of stars, before, with a sigh, she got slowly into her truck and drove home.

At Googon, the next day trailed like a week. Most of it
Sherry spent outside with the men, getting through her
usual share of work. Scott never came near, nor did he
ring, although when she got in that evening, Leda told
her that Mrs Armstrong had rung twice.

'How is Scott?' asked Mary, without preamble, when
Sherry rang back.

Sherry swallowed in an attempt to speak normally. 'I
saw him last night and he—he doesn't seem too bad.'

'Oh.' Mary paused, sounding disappointed when
Sherry didn't add anything, 'I—well, I did think you'd
have more to tell me than that!'

Such as what? Sherry wondered bleakly. 'Why don't
you go and see him yourself?' she suggested.

Again Mary hesitated. 'Simon and I thought of it,
but when I rang, Mrs Fox said Dulcie Easten was
visiting and would probably be there all day, and a little
of Dulcie goes a long way!'

'As long as Scott's happy,' Sherry said flatly.

'Somehow,' Mary answered caustically, 'I can't see
him improving much with her around!'

Going slowly to shower, before beginning to help
Leda with dinner, Sherry felt increasingly chilled, the
only sensation left in her breast that of pain. So Dulcie
was with him after all. Oh, it was tempting to believe
she could have called without being invited, as Sherry
had done herself, last night, but only Scott could have
asked her to stay all day. He hadn't been in touch with
Googon and he wasn't sick enough to be unable to pick
up a phone. This must be his way of letting her know
that what had happened between them had meant
nothing to him and it was Dulcie who really held a firm
place in his affections. Sherry knew she had behaved
foolishly and indiscreetly, but it was a lesson well
learned. How horrified Mary would have been if she
had said to her, 'I gave myself to him and now he
doesn't want me.'

Late the following afternoon, she received a short

missive from Kim. As she recognised his handwriting,
Sherry's frozen heart warmed. She had been feeling
curiously deserted. A letter from Kim, no matter how
brief, reminded her that she wasn't entirely alone in the
world.

She had opened it and was halfway through it before
she realised she was slowly freezing again. 'It can't be
true!' she gasped aloud, and began to re-read, but it
seemed worse the second time. Numbly she wondered
how she could have imagined it might be better.
Blinking her burning eyes, she tried to take it in.

Kim was selling Googon. He had met this girl—he
referred to her as a high-class bird—who didn't go for
men who lived in shabby bed-sitters. Harold Gibson, he
went on, was fair but stingy. On his present salary it
might be years before he could afford anything decent
in the way of accommodation, and, he declared, apart
from anything else, he had had enough discomfort in
Australia to last him a lifetime. After Googon was sold,
he concluded, Sherry should be able to find work in
either Sydney or Melbourne. He was still of the opinion
that there was nothing for her in London, but if she did
get stuck, she was to let him know.

Sherry felt so shaken that when Leda came to find
her in the living-room, she asked anxiously if there was
anything wrong. Sherry didn't answer directly. Wiping
a tear from her cheek, she shook her head hastily. 'I'm
going out again, Leda, I don't know for how long.'

Taking the truck, she turned in the direction of the
river, driving blindly towards a favourite spot. She found
it with the ease of long practice, a deep ravine, a few miles
from the house. She pulled up beside some stunted trees
and left the truck to sit under their leafy branches. Quite
often it was beautiful here, but, today, everything was
brown and withered in the terrifying heat. The grass was
so dry that the wind blowing through it made it crackle,
and Sherry wondered how long it might be before the
devastating flames arrived from the south to swallow it up.

She watched the dull flow of the Darling with lustreless eyes, forcing herself painfully to consider the unenviable situation she was in. She felt terribly let down, both by Scott and Kim, though she had to admit what had happened at Coomarlee had been her own fault. Scott hadn't tried to get in touch with her and Dulcie had moved in. He must now consider her an embarrassment, if he ever thought of her at all, and no doubt would be relieved to hear she was leaving Googon.

The thing was, where could she go? She supposed she could stay for a while with Mary and Simon, but that wouldn't really solve anything. It might be better to do as Kim suggested and find something farther afield. Kim didn't mention money but she was sure he would leave her enough to see her through until she found a job? As a sob escaped her, she told herself severely not to be so self-pitying. She must be a lot better off than those who had lost everything in the terrible fires. The future might look grey and grim, but there must be a niche for her somewhere. Hadn't the idea of caring for people always appealed to her? Perhaps she could train as a nurse?

Despite trying to convince herself, with false humour, that all was not lost, another sob rose in her throat. This time she didn't try to fight it but flung herself wearily on the hard, baked ground and cried until she fell asleep. Her last vague thoughts were that she might feel better if she let some of the grief wash out of her system, instead of bottling it up.

It was like this that Scott found her, curled in a small, pathetic ball, her face still hot and damp with tears. He had followed her tracks with comparative ease, yet there was grim relief in his eyes as he stood looking down on her and several bitter curses on his lips. Then, sinking to her side with a smothered exclamation, he drew her carefully into his arms and gently shook her awake.

Sherry thought she must still be dreaming when she lifted heavy lashes and found herself gazing straight in Scott's eyes, 'Scott,' she whispered uncertainly, 'what are you doing here?'

His mouth tightened as her soft lips trembled. 'I came to find you.'

'It's not that,' she swallowed in an effort to speak clearly, to try to come to terms with the shock of wakening up and finding herself in his arms. 'I've been so dreadfully worried. You were hurt, you might have been killed. I never even asked how you were, and I've had the most terrible dreams . . .'

'Hush!' he broke through her feverish incoherence huskily, his arms drawing her protectively closer. 'I'm all right now, so are you, and from now on I'll keep you safe.'

'Safe?' His words penetrated oddly. 'How can you?'

'We're going to be married,' he said firmly, 'in a few days' time. I'll have every right to look after you then.'

Sherry's eyes filled with agonising tears. Scott wasn't asking if she would marry him; he was giving her no choice! She had always realised he wasn't a man to plead and argue, and in this respect he would never change. He had a lot of pride, though, and would never consider marriage lightly. It must be because of what had happened that he felt forced to ask a girl like her to be his wife. He would believe he must do the honourable thing.

'You—you can't marry me, Scott,' she stammered, her cheeks hot, 'Wh-what happened was as much my fault as yours.'

Grimly his brows rose. 'You mean when we made love?'

Clenching taut hands, she nodded. 'I wanted you as much as you wanted me.'

His eyes darkened for a moment, as if he remembered. 'That has nothing to do with my proposal of marriage,' he said softly. 'That merely convinced me of what I'd already suspected, that I'll be getting a very responsive wife.'

Torn by shame, Sherry tried to push him away. 'I'll never know, will I? If I agreed to be your wife, I'd always feel you married me because you felt it was the right thing to do.'

'Sherry!' he exclaimed impatiently, still holding her in the circle of his powerful arms. 'If I told you I loved you, cared for you as I've never cared for anyone else, would you believe me?'

Her eyes, a troubled, clouded blue, cleared with a transparent kind of wonder. She knew he would never lie over something like that. 'Yes,' she breathed, 'I would.'

'Yes,' he said. 'Well, I do.'

She stared at him, realising incredulously that it was love she saw stamped on that proud, hard face. A strong, wholly encompassing, demanding love that might never change. And yet—'I still find it difficult to believe you intended marrying me,' she gulped.

Scott lifted his head, his eyes holding a compelling gleam of triumph. 'What would you say if I told you that I wanted to marry you long before I went away? If I could offer proof?'

'Proof?' she whispered.

'Yes, my little doubting Thomasina!' he growled, regarding her arrogantly. 'Simon Armstrong wouldn't tell you, because I asked him not to, but when the fires broke out in the south, I rang and asked him to look after you. I told him you were the girl I hoped to marry and exactly what I would do to him should he let anything happen to my future wife.'

Sherry felt a tremor run right through her. 'Oh, Scott!' she moaned, but suddenly, as though hungry for the touch of her lips, he pulled her tightly against him and began kissing her deeply, cutting off further words. Lacing his hands through her hair, he tilted her head back so his mouth could part hers, at first almost fiercely, then with a relentless gentleness that was equally ravishing. And all the time Sherry clung to him, feeling at peace but unbearably stirred and excited.

'Now do you believe?' he asked.

She nodded, raising starry blue eyes which were trusting yet reproachful. 'Why didn't you say anything before?'

Knowing what she meant, he replied wryly, 'They told me I was mad when I discharged myself from hospital, and by the time I got home I was nearly ready to believe it. I'd had a rest when you came, though. In fact, I was considering coming to see you, and when you walked in it was perhaps a culmination of many things, but I completely lost control. It had never happened before, although with you, I've often felt my restraint slipping. And when I woke you were gone and my head was so bad I couldn't even get as far as the door to come after you.'

'If only you'd rung,' she whispered, recalling the anguish she'd gone through.

'I didn't want it like that, Sherry,' Scott said flatly. 'The next time I saw you I had to be able to deal with everything. It also seemed to me that you hadn't been able to get away fast enough, and I believed I must give you time to be sure of your feelings.'

'I was—I am—I love you!' Sherry cried incoherently, pressing soft little kisses on his mouth and hard cheeks. 'Oh, darling, when you didn't come and Mary said Dulcie was with you . . .'

'Did she indeed?' His mouth quirked as he returned Sherry's kisses in good measure. 'Mary was probably wondering what was going on and trying to help me by making you jealous. Dulcie only stayed long enough to hear, very finally, that she was wasting her time.'

'She—she once told me,' Sherry swallowed, 'that you'd had an affair.'

'Nonsense! We were never lovers,' he replied with brutal frankness. 'Occasionally I took her out when I needed a partner, but I never let her think I had any serious intentions.'

'But you let me think!' Sherry looked at him reproachfully again.

Scott said wryly, 'I believe I was also trying to arouse a little jealousy in your seemingly immune breast. There I was seething with it, every time you so much as looked at another man, while nothing I did appeared to bother you at all. You responded when I kissed you, but I thought it was only physical, and I wanted more than that.'

'I didn't even know you liked me,' Sherry confessed with considerable awe.

His brows drew together darkly. 'I've been conscious of you since you first came to Googon, when I considered you were still a child, but it wasn't until we were alone together in Brisbane that I realised you were the woman I'd been looking for all my life. But it wasn't easy to admit it, even to myself. Despite what I'd told you, I hadn't planned on getting married again and I couldn't decide what to do about you.'

His voice was so matter-of-fact she felt a quiver of amusement even as she managed to note severely, 'It seemed very clear what you intended doing about me. After Kim left, you suggested immediately that I should follow him!'

Scott laughed. 'That was for your sake, not mine. If you'd taken my advice, I shouldn't have been long in coming after you. I may have said some unpleasant things, but you must admit I was provoked. Deserted by your brother, you wouldn't let me take over, and it actually hurt me to see you growing so thin.'

Sherry flushed and confessed, 'I was glad of your support, though I pretended not to be. It was because I loved you so much that I believed I'd be wiser to see as little of you as possible. I never imagined you would ever love me.'

His mouth crushed hers again to confirm it, then,

lifting her chin, he stared deep into her bemused eyes. 'You won't ever have a reason to run from me again,' he said gently.

Suddenly Sherry remembered. She stiffened and went cold. 'I don't know how I could have forgotten!' she gasped, 'When I came here, I wasn't really running from you. I had a letter from Kim . . .'

'I know,' Scott cut in, his face darkening grimly, 'I found it and read it. You'll have to forgive me, but if I'd been able to get my hands on Kim there and then, he wouldn't have lived to enjoy his ill-gotten gains. Eventually,' he continued harshly, 'I might be able to forgive him, but I warn you, it might take years.'

Somehow, though she felt no bitterness, Sherry was content not to argue. In time they might all get together again, but Kim had treated her callously and she refused to worry about him any more.

She heard Scott saying, 'I'll put in an offer for Googon, darling. If we get it, Sam can stay on as manager. I think, your grandfather would like it kept in the family.'

'Oh, yes,' she smiled gratefully.

'Not that he wasn't at fault either,' Scott added in clipped tones. 'Did he pay you anything for all the work he made you do?'

'It doesn't matter,' she said quickly, unwilling to dwell on the past, now there was such a wonderful future to look forward to.

Scott captured her hand, kissing her soft little palm. 'You're very forgiving and loving, aren't you?'

Her cheeks flushed with rosy colour as she wondered what he was hinting at. 'The other night——' she began haltingly.

'That was only the beginning,' he broke in, tracing the line of her quivering lip with a seductive finger. 'My love, I didn't even begin to show you what it's going to be like between us. I think my strength gave out almost before I got started!'

Disregarding the wryness of his tones, she murmured in entrancing confusion, 'It was—beautiful, darling.'

He drew her closer, his eyes smouldering. 'I'll show you it can be that and more. It will be wildly exciting, so wonderful you won't ever regret marrying me. You, my darling child, arouse feelings in me I've never felt before. If you ever imagined I'd give you up, you must have been crazy!'

'It was you!' Sherry reminded him in breathless indignation. 'You kept telling me I wasn't good enough for you ...'

'Well, I had to erect some form of defence,' he smiled, 'and that seemed as good a way as any. As long as you were angry with me I felt fairly safe.'

'Oh, darling, I was never that angry.' She looked at him remorsefully, then her voice trailed off incredulously.

'What is it?' he asked quickly, staring down on her startled face.

'Clouds?' she whispered, in awe-stricken tones. 'Clouds!'

Scott glanced upwards and sure enough, there were huge formations of greyish black clouds cutting out the sun, and even as he nodded in satisfied understanding, great drops of rain began falling on their upturned faces.

'It's raining!' Sherry exclaimed, almost unable to articulate.

Scott nodded soberly, much of the underlying grimness easing from his strong features. 'It started in the south—I heard just as I was leaving Coomarlee I was going to tell you, but now all I can say is, thank God!'

Sherry could see he was remembering the dreadful tragedy of the past weeks and wouldn't easily forget. With infinite compassion she slid her arms round his shoulders, lightly caressing the back of his neck, trying to convey how she felt. 'There'll be much more you can do. That we can do together, once we're married,' she said.

He smiled, a great warmth and tenderness in his eyes as he regarded her. 'I'm taking you to stay with Mary and Simon for the two days before our wedding,' he murmured huskily. 'Then I'll be able to spend a lifetime proving how much I adore you.'

He might be taking her to the Armstrongs', but, although he drew her gently to her feet, he didn't appear to be in a great hurry. And as he lifted her face to look at her, what she saw in his eyes made her catch her breath.

'I love you,' he said simply, then began kissing her.

Sherry clung to him, returning kisses that deepened swiftly to passion, her heart racing in tune with his. He held her closely, so she could feel every urgent bone of his powerful body pressed against her, and it was, for Sherry, one of the most wonderful things she had ever experienced, to be standing here, in this sun-baked land, being kissed by the man she loved and getting steadily soaked by the now heavily falling rain.

She would stay in Australia, she thought dreamily. Scott's land would become her land, and perhaps, one day, their children might grow up to love it as they did.

A long time later her mouth curved in a smile of rapture as she looked up into his face. 'Oh, Scott,' was all she could say, trying to tell him but her heart almost too full for words. She leaned against him, her head in the hollow of his shoulder, letting his passionate murmurs of love flow over her, feeling utterly content. Then, as he turned her tenderly from the river, she slipped her arm round his waist and together they made their way slowly back home.

H·A·R·L·E·Q·U·I·N

FIRST·CLASS
Sweepstakes

OFFICIAL RULES

1. NO PURCHASE NECESSARY. To enter, complete the official entry/order form. Be sure to indicate whether or not you wish to take advantage of our subscription offer.

2. Entry blanks have been preselected for the prizes offered. Your response will be checked to see if you are a winner. In the event that these preselected responses are not claimed, a random drawing will be held from all entries received to award not less than $150,000 in prizes. This is in addition to any free, surprise or mystery gifts which might be offered. Versions of this sweepstakes with different prizes will appear in Preview Service Mailings by Harlequin Books and their affiliates. Winners selected will receive the prize offered in their sweepstakes brochure.

3. This promotion is being conducted under the supervision of Marden-Kane, an independent judging organization. By entering the sweepstakes, each entrant accepts and agrees to be bound by these rules and the decisions of the judges, which shall be final and binding. Odds of winning in the random drawing are dependent upon the total number of entries received. Taxes, if any, are the sole responsibility of the prize winners. Prizes are nontransferable. All entries must be received by August 31, 1986.

4. The following prizes will be awarded:

    (1) Grand Prize: Rolls-Royce™ *or* $100,000 Cash!
                       (Rolls-Royce being offered by permission of
                       Rolls-Royce Motors Inc.)

    (1) Second Prize: A trip for two to Paris for 7 days/6 nights. Trip includes air transportation on the Concorde, hotel accommodations...PLUS...$5,000 spending money!

    (1) Third Prize: A luxurious Mink Coat!

5. This offer is open to residents of the U.S. and Canada, 18 years or older, except employees of Harlequin Books, its affiliates, subsidiaries, Marden-Kane and all other agencies and persons connected with conducting this sweepstakes. All Federal, State and local laws apply. Void in the province of Quebec and wherever prohibited or restricted by law. Winners will be notified by mail and may be required to execute an affidavit of eligibility and release, which must be returned within 14 days after notification. Canadian winners will be required to answer a skill-testing question. Winners consent to the use of their name, photograph and/or likeness for advertising and publicity purposes in conjunction with this and similar promotions without additional compensation. One prize per family or household.

6. For a list of our most current prize winners, send a stamped, self-addressed envelope to: WINNERS LIST, c/o Marden-Kane, P.O. Box 10404, Long Island City, New York 11101

Here's how to get this special offer from Harlequin! As simple as 1...2...3!

SEPTEMBER
TREASURY EDITION
COUPON

1. Each month, save one Treasury Edition coupon from your favorite Romance or Presents novel.
2. In four months you'll have saved four Treasury Edition coupons (<u>only one coupon per month allowed</u>).
3. Then all you have to do is fill out and return the order form provided, along with the four Treasury Edition coupons required and $1.00 for postage and handling.

Mail to: Harlequin Reader Service

In the U.S.A.
2504 West Southern Ave.
Tempe, AZ 85282

In Canada
P.O. Box 2800, Postal Station A
5170 Yonge Street
Willowdale, Ont. M2N 6J3

RT1-B-2

Please send me my FREE copy of the Janet Dailey Treasury Edition. I have enclosed the four Treasury Edition coupons required and $1.00 for postage and handling along with this order form.

(Please Print)

NAME_____

ADDRESS_____

CITY_____

STATE/PROV. _____ ZIP/POSTAL CODE_____

SIGNATURE_____

This offer is limited to one order per household.

SUPPLIES LIMITED

This special Janet Dailey offer expires January 1986.

*You're invited to accept
4 books and a
surprise gift* **Free!**

Acceptance Card

Mail to: **Harlequin Reader Service®**

In the U.S.
2504 West Southern Ave.
Tempe, AZ 85282

In Canada
P.O. Box 2800, Postal Station A
5170 Yonge Street
Willowdale, Ontario M2N 6J3

YES! Please send me 4 free Harlequin Presents® novels and my free surprise gift. Then send me 8 brand new novels every month as they come off the presses. Bill me at the low price of $1.75 each ($1.95 in Canada)—an 11% saving off the retail price. There are no shipping, handling or other hidden costs. There is no minimum number of books I must purchase. I can always return a shipment and cancel at any time. Even if I never buy another book from Harlequin, the 4 free novels and the surprise gift are mine to keep forever.   108 BPP-BPGE

_____

Name   (PLEASE PRINT)

_____

Address   Apt. No.

_____

City   State/Prov.   Zip/Postal Code

This offer is limited to one order per household and not valid to present subscribers. Price is subject to change.   ACP-SUB-1